WILKIN'S GHOST

ALSO BY ROBERT BURCH

D.J.'S WORST ENEMY

DOODLE AND THE GO-CART

*HUT SCHOOL AND THE
WARTIME HOME-FRONT HEROES*

JOEY'S CAT

QUEENIE PEAVY

RENFROE'S CHRISTMAS

SKINNY

TWO THAT WERE TOUGH

TYLER, WILKIN, AND SKEE

WILKIN'S GHOST

ROBERT BURCH

Illustrated by Lloyd Bloom

THE VIKING PRESS, NEW YORK

G917326

First Edition
Text Copyright © Robert Burch, 1978
Illustrations Copyright © Viking Penguin Inc., 1978
All rights reserved
First published in 1978 by The Viking Press
625 Madison Avenue, New York, N.Y. 10022
Published simultaneously in Canada by
Penguin Books Canada Limited
Printed in U.S.A.
1 2 3 4 5 82 81 80 79 78

Library of Congress Cataloging in Publication Data
Burch, Robert, Wilkin's Ghost.
Summary: A boy living in rural Georgia in 1935 befriends
an accused teenage thief he believes is innocent.
[1. Georgia—Fiction. 2. Friendship—Fiction]
I. Bloom, Lloyd. II. Title.
PZ7.B91585Wi   [Fic]   78–6293
ISBN 0–670–76897–9

jB
8934
wiL

for Howard, Wilson, and Julia Burch

Contents

WILKIN'S GHOST

1

The Hanging Tree

"I wouldn't go near the hanging tree at a time like this for a million dollars," said Big Will after the first clap of thunder. He looked at me. "You better stick with us, Wilkin."

"I wouldn't go near it when there's a storm brewing for *two* million dollars," said his wife, Edna.

And my brother Skee said, "I wouldn't go near it for ten million."

Six-year-old Katie, Edna and Big Will's daughter, said, "Why, I wouldn't even go near it for a hundred dollars."

The rest of us laughed. "I mean a thousand dollars,"

she said, and when we laughed more she screamed, "I mean a hundred thousand million!"

"There, Daughter," said Big Will, patting her on the head, "that's better! If you're gonna outwhopper the rest of us, you gotta do it right!"

We were walking along the main road, and I had said that I planned to take a shortcut through the woods ahead. The only trouble was that the shortcut went past the hanging tree.

We heard the whistle of the six o'clock train as it was pulling out of the station at Blyden's Crossing, a mile away. "Let's hurry," said Edna. "Maybe we'll beat the train." She meant that maybe we'd get up the hill and across the tracks before it came along. But we were too tired to hurry. We'd picked squash all afternoon and then washed and sorted them.

Suddenly it was getting so dark that I was sorry I'd mentioned I would take the shortcut. This was no time to be in the woods by myself. "Don't you want to go through the woods?" I asked my other brother, Tyler. "We'll get home a heap quicker."

"Not this time," said Tyler. Tyler is fourteen, a year older than I am, and he's the most level-headed one of us. I should have known when he didn't choose to go through the woods that it wasn't the thing to do. Skee is younger; he's ten. I knew there was no use in asking him to come. He's so sociable that he'd rather be with as many people as possible. Also, he's musical, and Big Will had been teaching him to harmonize while we were finishing up the work at the grading shed. During the summer we help Mr. Madden, a produce farmer, whenever he needs extra hands. Big Will is a farmer too, but his main crop is cotton, and the work's caught up on that for a few weeks. He's glad to have extra work, and of course my two brothers and I are always glad to get paying jobs. We have plenty of jobs keeping up with the chores at home, but they don't bring in cash for us.

I knew that Skee hoped to sing with Big Will the rest of the way home, but I asked anyway, "How about you, Skee? Come the shortcut. Maybe we'll see some snakes."

"I wouldn't be caught dead going near that ol' hanging tree when there's liable to be a storm."

"It's because there's liable to be a storm," I argued, "that I want to get home in a hurry."

"Not me," he said. "Not bad enough to go through there." He pointed toward the woods. "And anyway, me and Big Will might just sing us a few songs."

Big Will laughed, and Edna said, "That's a good idea. You and Will sing, and maybe you'll hold back the clouds till we can get home!"

The train was coming just as we got to the crossing, and we waited for it to pass. I hoped Miss Etta and Miss Julia would be sitting on the side nearest us, but they weren't. We saw them on the other side, looking out the window. Miss Etta and Miss Julia are our neighbors, and they were taking the train to Manchester to spend a few days since Miss Etta had time off from her job at the canning plant. While they were away my brothers and I were to tend their livestock, feed the cat, and even sleep in their rambling old house. "To keep the boogers from

: 5 :

carrying it away!" Miss Etta had said as a joke when she'd asked us if we'd stay. I'd been doing the milking for them for more than a year, so helping at their place was nothing new to me.

The train moved on, and a man standing at the end of it waved to us. I wished I were on the train going someplace too. I wished it whenever I saw the train—no matter which direction it was going. I liked home well enough, but at the same time I wished lots of times that I could see more than just what was nearby.

We crossed the tracks and were almost to my turning-off place—if I planned to keep to the notion of taking the shortcut. Naturally I planned to keep to it. When I say I'll do something I usually do it. That's because I've got determination. Tyler and Skee call it stubbornness. Still, I started to change my mind, but they'd have said that I was afraid of the hanging tree too. That's what we call the giant hickory at the other end of the woods where the trail comes out, near Miss Etta's and Miss Julia's house. A man had been hanged from it ten years ago.

Old-timers still talk about the hanging. It took place during a thunderstorm, and some people believe that the man's ghost still comes out every time there's a storm. According to them, it dances about under the tree just itching for somebody to come along.

"That ghost has been seeking revenge since 1925," warned Edna. "If I was you, Wilkin, I wouldn't go that way."

"I'm not afraid," I said, although it didn't exactly cheer me to remember stories I'd heard about the ghost.

: 6 :

There were people who claimed to have seen it during storms, but I don't believe in such things. Lightning plays strange tricks, and things can look like they're moving about during an electrical storm when it's nothing more than flickering light. At least that's my explanation.

"You'd better stay with us," urged Edna.

"The hanging took place a long time ago," I argued. "And the man was a bootlegger who'd been feuding with other bootleggers. If his ghost is after revenge, it ought to go looking for whisky-makers to pester instead of farm folks like us."

"That's what I say," said Big Will, which made me feel better. Then he added, "I say that, and you say that, but the ghost, he don't say nothin' like that. He says, 'Give me revenge! Give me revenge!'" His voice was low and eerie. He repeated, "Give me revenge! Give me revenge!"

A cold feeling came over me, and I almost shivered. "Let the ghost say it to me!" I said, sounding braver than I felt, just as we came to the trail that was the beginning of the shortcut. "Come on, Ally Greevy," I called, whistling for our dog. At least I'd have him for company. He came running—a trip into the woods was always to his liking. But he looked around, puzzled, when nobody else followed us. I could tell that he was undecided about what to do. "Come on!" I said, urging him to go with me. "You'll like this way better!" But partway down the trail he turned and ran back to the road. He's like Skee, so sociable that he has to be with the crowd.

Everyone on the road laughed when he went back to join them. "He's got better sense than to go near the hanging tree too!" yelled Skee. The others laughed again, but that only increased my determination to go through the woods. I pretended I hadn't heard, but I was disgusted with Ally Greevy. I hoped I could remember being mad at him till the next time he wanted me to do something for him—sneak an extra biscuit for him from the kitchen cupboard or throw sticks for him to fetch.

The sky was turning darker, and there was a bolt of lightning. It didn't scare me, but I nearly jumped over a tree stump when the thunder rolled. It sounded as if every tree in the woods were falling in on me. Then things were quiet, and the next sound I heard was singing. Skee and Big Will were trying to blend their voices on "The Music Goes 'Round and 'Round," a new song they had heard on the radio. Skee and Big Will always keep up on new songs. They sang this one loud, as if they thought they really could hold back the storm.

The woods on the hillside are fairly open, but they were so dark now that I dreaded getting to the part where the trees are thicker and the undergrowth is dense. It occurred to me that I should turn back, but I kept going. Maybe Skee and Tyler were right; maybe I was too stubborn to ever change my mind.

"It's determination," I said out loud, just to hear a sound. The singing had faded away, and between claps of thunder the woods were deathly quiet. I walked fast —I might become scared if I slowed down enough to think about what I was doing. At the same time I told myself there was nothing to be afraid of. Determination and a moderate amount of courage had seen me through bad times before, and I was not about to let a ghost, or tales of a ghost, scare me . . . much.

2

Storm

Deep in the woods there's a fast-flowing stream. Where the trail crosses it, the water runs in and out of rocky places and makes a gurgling noise. I once made the mistake of calling it a babbling brook after reading about such things in a story. Tyler and Skee had kept me reminded of it. "Wilkin's Babbling Brook," they'd say. Sometimes it made me mad to be teased about it and we'd get into fights. Other times I'd go along with the joke— even adding to it, which stopped their teasing quicker than hitting them. The last time they'd brought up the subject, I'd said, "Yes, the stream flows rhythmically onward until it reaches watery depths of brine."

"What does all that mean?" Skee asked.

Tyler answered, "It means the creek keeps going till it stops."

"Is that all?"

"No," I said. "It means it goes till it empties into the ocean."

"Say it again, Wilkin," Skee said, but Tyler asked me to kindly wait till he wasn't around or he might throw up.

My babbling brook didn't sound so pleasant when a storm was closing in, but I was pleased to be starting across it. At least I'd be that much nearer home. Also, I was pleased that it had not started to rain.

The vines hanging from tree branches overhead were so thick that I could see only a patch of sky, and it was the darkest gray I had ever seen. Instead of wading, I decided to cross the stream by stepping from one rock to another. I'd done it often in the past.

Maybe I was in too much of a hurry, or maybe it was because I couldn't see as well as usual—clouds helping the treetops and vines to shut out daylight—that I missed my footing. I landed in a sitting-up position on the rocky bottom of the stream.

Nothing was harmed but my self-confidence, and I got up and shook myself good, like a dog that has taken a swim, and waded to the opposite bank. Ferns covered the ground on both sides of the trail, and before I'd taken two steps there was a streak of lightning across the little bit of sky that I could see. Immediately afterwards there was a streak of something across the trail in front of me.

I'd heard of lightning plowing a furrow in the ground, but I'd never seen it happen. I jumped back, and then I realized it wasn't lightning: it was a snake, a poisonous moccasin, crossing from the ferns on one side of the trail to the other. I knew there were snakes around; Tyler, Skee, and I sometimes hunted them, poking about in the greenery near the stream with big sticks. But I didn't have a big stick with me or the time to be interested in a snake. I'd just as soon not see any more wildlife.

At that moment it began to rain, and I hurried along the trail. I didn't mind getting wetter, but the rain made it difficult to see. I had trouble keeping to the trail, and after a while I realized that I hadn't kept to it. I stumbled around but couldn't tell where or when I'd gone wrong.

It came to me that I could wait till the storm was over, and then I could find my way out. But if the storm lasted long, it would be night when it was over. Without a light I might not get home till after daybreak.

I hoped the storm wouldn't last long, but there was no way of telling whether it would or not. Two weeks ago we'd had a terrible storm in the afternoon. It got so dark that chickens went to roost, thinking it was night. Half an hour later the storm was over, the sun was out, and the chickens were scratching around outdoors. Maybe they thought it was a new day. I don't know what they thought an hour later when the sun set and it was night sure enough, but I knew that now I'd better keep moving through the woods.

I stumbled over bushes and fallen logs and almost ran into trees that I couldn't see because of the blinding rain.

Once I fell into a big hole where a stump had rotted out, and any number of times I ran into brier thickets. The thorns tore through my overalls as if I didn't have on anything at all.

After a long while of making my way a few steps at a time, the rain eased up. Then there was a flash of lightning that lit up the woods. I thought I saw a figure jump behind the trunk of a big tree ahead, and I hurried toward it. I was certain that it was just one of those illusions, part lightning and part imagination, that appear to be something they're not.

The rain started again, an even heavier downpour than earlier, but in the next flash of lightning I saw that I was back on the trail. Then I realized that I was heading toward the hanging tree.

I thought of going past it, but I nagged at myself: If I didn't believe in ghosts, why was I scared? Still, I started to run. Nobody but me would ever know that I hadn't dared stop under it. But I was scratched from tangling with the briers, and bruised from the sprawls I'd taken in getting through underbrush. Too tired to run and almost too weary to be afraid, I took a deep breath and walked under the hanging tree. For some silly reason I balled up one fist as if I expected to take a punch at the ghost. Underneath the tree I leaned against its giant trunk to rest.

Although it was wet there, the big branches overhead caught some of the water, and it ran down them and off their tips. It fell to the ground along the outer branches as if it were a curtain. I guessed this was the way water-

falls looked from hollow spaces behind them.

I propped one foot back of me against the trunk of the tree, glad for the protection of its sheltering boughs. Lightning crackled in the limbs overhead, and it came to me that the tallest tree in the woods does not provide the safest shelter during a storm. Maybe lightning in the top of this one was what had caused the stories to get started about a ghost that came out during storms.

Then I remembered the figure I thought I'd seen jumping behind the tree, and I wanted to find out what it might have been. It was probably only a dead limb propped against the other side, and flickering light on it had made it appear to jump. But when I started to move, I had a strange feeling—a feeling that I was not alone.

I wanted to look behind me, but something caused me to hesitate. Sound reasoning prompted me to think it was just tales I'd heard about the ghost that made me think something was there, but I didn't get much satisfaction from sound reasoning at that moment. To egg myself on and to hear my voice when it was hemmed in by all the rain, I said out loud, "I'm coming around there to get you, Ghost!" It was like being in a little room with all the doors and windows closed; the sound seemed to stay close in. My voice had been a bit shaky, so I decided to say something else. This time I tried to sound like the Troll frightening the Billy Goats Gruff. In a low voice I said, "If you're still under this tree when I get around there, Ghost, I'm gonna kick you in the pants!"

At that I felt better, but the feeling didn't last. Suddenly there was a noise like twigs breaking underfoot. I knew that something was running away. I sprang back from the trunk of the tree and looked around.

Something was dashing through the curtain of rain on the opposite side and running into the woods. I barely glimpsed it beyond sheets of rain as it disappeared into a pine thicket. All I could see was a flicker of something white—or a ghost.

3

The Way of a Ghost

I wished more than ever that Ally Greevy had come along. If whatever I'd seen run into the woods was real, then I could have said, "Get 'em, Ally Greevy! Go get 'em!" and he'd have chased down anything, storm or no storm.

I didn't know what to do besides shiver till it came to me that whatever had been there was afraid of me. On hearing me say that I was going to come around to the other side of the tree, it had run away.

There was another flash of lightning, and I glimpsed the bit of white again. Without thinking too much about it, I decided to give chase; otherwise I'd never know what it was. I think I had in mind now that it would be a deer. The white I'd seen would have been its tail as it ran away. I knew I wouldn't be able to catch a deer unless it was as blinded by the rain as I was, which wasn't likely, but in the next flash of lightning I saw the white again, and it was bigger than the tail of any deer. It looked for all the world like a ghost, but still it was running away. If it had been a ghost seeking revenge, running away from me was no way to get it.

The rain beat down, and I tripped over a mass of honeysuckle vines and sprawled on the ground. Soon I was up and running again. The white thing was getting farther away, but I kept my eyes on it as best I could and stayed on its trail. Vines tripped me another time, and once I got tangled in blackberry brambles. While I was pulling away from them I lost sight of the ghost, but soon I saw it again—way in the distance—and I ran after it.

The rain kept pouring down and I kept running, occasionally glimpsing the white thing. I followed it as if it were a flag signaling me on. Finally I didn't see it anywhere, which was all right with me because I was too exhausted to keep running. In a few minutes the rain slowed down to a drizzle. Then the sky began to lighten, and I could see clearly where I was standing. I almost fainted.

I was at the edge of an old, abandoned well. I'd known it was in the woods; Tyler, Skee, and I had come across it every now and then. Pa'd put logs across it once to keep anybody from accidentally falling into it and drowning. But the logs had rotted out, and now there

:19:

was a gaping hole in the earth. If I had taken one more step, I would have fallen into it. It made me weak just to think about such a thing. The ghost had almost tricked me into running smack into a death trap. Maybe that's how a ghost gets revenge. Maybe that's the way of a ghost.

I started out of the woods then, wanting to get away in a hurry. Tired as I was, it was amazing how much strength I found to make a fast exit. By the time I reached home, the clouds were gone and the sun, although it was nearly time for it to set, was shining.

Skee was in the backyard shelling corn for the chickens. He said, "I thought you were gonna get home before we did; I thought that's why you took the shortcut."

"I thought so too," I said, going into the house.

Tyler was in the kitchen talking to Mamma, who was cooking supper. "We've been home a long time," he said. "We were at Big Will's and Edna's before the storm broke loose, and we stayed there till it slacked up." Big Will and his family live about halfway between our house and Mr. Madden's.

Mamma was frying salmon croquettes at the stove, and when she'd turned them over to brown on the other side, she looked at me. "My goodness, Wilkin," she said, "what happened to you?"

"I got scratched up."

"I see you did," she said, handing a spatula to Tyler. "Here, keep the croquettes from burning while I find the iodine bottle."

I followed her into the next room, protesting the use

: 20 :

of iodine. Anyway, the scratches weren't bad. Iodine burned, and I didn't like having it put on me. "Roy Evans' mother uses Mercurochrome. She put some on Roy and me when we got skinned up one day." Roy is a friend of mine who lives in town, and I see him more during the school term than I do in summer. Mamma didn't say anything. She kept dressing my wounds, which didn't really burn much, but I flinched whenever she dabbed at them with more iodine. "Why can't we use Mercurochrome?" I asked.

"Roy's mother uses what she thinks best, and I use what I think best," she said, swatting me on the seat to let me know the doctoring was over. "Hurry, now, and get the milking done at Miss Julia's. We'll be ready to eat when your pa comes home." Pa's job at the sawmill is hard work, and he's always hungry at suppertime.

I dreaded having to go past the hanging tree again on the way to Miss Julia's and Miss Etta's barn. I even dreaded going into their kitchen for the milking utensils. Their house is so far back in a grove of trees that it seems cut off from the rest of the world. Lots of times when I was there I didn't see either of the women. I'd get the utensils and head to the barn, and afterwards I'd strain the milk in their big kitchen and come home—but I always knew they were around someplace. At least I always knew that Miss Julia was there; she almost never went off. Miss Etta worked at the canning plant and was gone part of the time. But today neither of them would be around.

Going back through the kitchen, I asked Tyler, "Don't

you want to go with me to do the milking? You haven't seen the new calf in a long time." The calf is our pay for doing the milking. The reason it's not just my pay is that Tyler does the milking for our family, and he and Skee double up on some of the other chores at home so that I can help our neighbors. That's why all of us are involved in the job, and our pay is the new calf each year. "Come on!" I urged Tyler. "Go with me!"

"I've got to cook supper," he said, and he and Mamma laughed. Of all of us, Tyler is the poorest help in the kitchen. It wouldn't have surprised me if the croquettes hadn't burned already.

Mamma said, "And anyway, Tyler must do our milking." Taking back the spatula, she said, "I'll see to this while you run on to the barn."

I started out, and in the backyard I asked Skee, "Have you finished your chores?"

"Almost," he said.

"Then go with me to do the milking."

"How come?"

" 'Cause you and Tyler get in on the pay," I said. "That's how come."

"We do your work here so you'll be able to do the work there."

"Well, it wouldn't hurt you to come help out occasionally. Anyway, lots of times you go along just to play with the calf."

"It ain't as playful as it was," he said, which was true. It's growing up. "And besides, the way you're begging me to go, you must be scared or something."

I knew better than to admit being scared, but I decided to be a little more open with him. "I saw something under the hanging tree," I confided.

"I reckon you'll expect me to believe it was the ghost."

"As a matter of fact, it was. And it nearly tricked me into falling into that old well down in the woods."

"Then I ain't about to go up there!" said Skee, and I walked away disgustedly.

When I was nearly to the road, he called, "But if you don't get back, I'll ask Pa to come up there and see what got you."

4

Night Sounds

Mollie, the Todd Sisters' cow, is usually so calm when I'm milking her that I wonder if she's gone to sleep. But this time she was jumpy. She lifted first one hoof and then another. She'd kick, and then she'd switch her tail. Once the end of it struck me on the back of my neck, stinging sharply. "Cut it out, will you?" I said. She swatted me again, and suddenly it occurred to me why she was fidgety: she'd seen the ghost too! Or maybe it was only the horseflies. The rain had driven them into the barn, and they were worrying her.

I turned the calf out of his stall, and he raced to his mother. While he was suckling I went to the Todds' kitchen to strain the milk. Knowing that I was the only one in the big house, so far from anyone else, made me feel more alone than I'd ever been. The place was ghostly quiet. I strained the milk, washed the utensils, and got out fast.

At the barn I pulled the calf away from the cow. "Come on, you've had your quota!" I said. "There'd be no milk left for anybody else if you had your way!" As usual, the lecture did not shame him; he jerked loose and dashed back to Mollie. With a little more force I persuaded him that he should return to his stall for the night.

Supper was ready when I got home, and while we were still at the table, Mr. Madden stopped by to ask if Tyler or I would go with him to Produce Row. He was taking the squash and might have to stay all night. We could help him watch for customers.

I wanted to go; it's always fun to go to Produce Row. But Pa said I was committed to look after things for the Todd Sisters. I didn't see why I was any more committed than my brothers, but Pa reminded me that I knew my way around their house better than anyone else. He said the women were counting on me.

So Tyler went to Produce Row, and I was sorry. I didn't begrudge him the trip, but I wished he'd been at home to go with Skee and me to the Todds'. Three of us against a ghost would be better than two.

When it was time to start to the house, Skee said, "I think I'll just stay at home tonight and sleep in my own bed."

"You *will not!*" I shouted.

"I will so."

"Now, boys!" said Mamma. "No arguments! And, Skee, I think maybe you should keep Wilkin company. You wouldn't want to sleep up there by yourself, would you?"

"I might," he said, "if I was as big as Wilkin. Anyway, I think I'll stay here."

Pa laughed. "Nothing's gonna get you, Skeedy-wo! Nothing'd have you!"

"But there might be a ghost in that big old house."

"Well, I should hope so!" said Pa. "Any house with character has a ghost!"

"Now, now!" said Mamma. "Let's be serious."

"Wilkin thought he saw a ghost during the storm," said Skee. "And it wasn't far from the house."

Mamma said, "Wilkin's too sensible to believe in such things." I wasn't sure I was *that* sensible, but I was glad she thought so. And I was glad that she made Skee go with me.

Inside the big house I took the flashlight and hunted for a lamp. The one on the kitchen table was out of kerosene. I'd have sworn it hadn't been empty when I'd glanced at it while straining the milk.

Skee stayed in the kitchen while I went into the dining room. Just as I reached for the lamp in the center of the table, I heard a noise in the front part of the house. I waited, expecting to hear it again, but nothing happened. I convinced myself it had only been my imagination—or a squirrel jumping onto the porch.

Back in the kitchen I lit the lamp. It was surprising how much better—and braver—I felt when there was a good light and someone else was near. "Maybe we just ought to walk up through the front rooms and see that everything's all right," I told Skee.

"Maybe we just ought to go crawl under the cover," he said. "Come on, let's go to bed."

I followed him through the little sitting room off to the side of the kitchen and into the back bedroom. The noise I'd heard must have been a squirrel.

Skee didn't waste time in getting to bed. He feels safe from any harm as long as he's covered up. Sometimes I'm understanding of his views, and this was one of them. It was a hot night, but I didn't argue with him when he wanted to pull a sheet over us.

Skee was soon snoring, but I couldn't go to sleep. I lay awake, thinking of what I'd seen at the hanging tree. I could hear the katydids and tree frogs outside. Suddenly the katydids and tree frogs were silent. It was as if they'd been performing on a radio that had been switched off. I wondered if something had scared them. Had the ghost floated across the yard and scared everything out there? Skee had stopped snoring. He was so quiet that I wasn't sure he was breathing. Everything was quiet. Then BLAM! There was a clanking noise in the kitchen.

I sprang up. As I pulled on my overalls, I listened for more racket, but there was none. "Skee!" I whispered.

: 27 :

"Skee! Wake up! Something's in the kitchen."

Skee didn't answer, and I shook him. "Huh?" he said. "What's the matter?"

"Somebody's in the house," I whispered.

"Yeah, me and you," he said sleepily.

"No, somebody else! I heard a loud noise in the kitchen."

"Did you really?" he asked. I could tell that he was wider awake now.

"And we're gonna catch whoever it is," I said firmly. "You take the flashlight but don't turn it on yet. Go through the sitting room to the kitchen, okay?"

"Where'll you be?" he asked.

"I'll go out in the side hall and around through the dining room. Don't shine your light till you're there. Can you feel your way in the dark?"

"Yeah, I guess." His voice was trembling, which didn't do anything to bolster my courage.

"I'll take the lamp," I whispered, feeling in my pocket to make certain that I had a match left. "We'll count slow to ourselves while we're making our way, and when we get to a hundred you ought to be at the side door of the kitchen and I'll be at the dining room. Then you turn on the flashlight and shine it around, and I'll light the lamp. All right?"

"Yeah, I guess."

"Okay, then let's go," I said. "One . . . two . . . three . . . four. . . ." I whispered the numbers at first, then counted to myself.

Holding one hand in front of me, I made my way

through the dark hallway. With my other hand I held the big lamp. By the time I'd counted to fifty I was still not out of the hall. I hated to think what would happen to the big lamp and me if I stumbled over anything. Fortunately, nothing was in my way and I arrived at the kitchen door on the count of 96. I drew a match from my pocket and counted to myself. "Ninety-seven, ninety-eight, ninety-nine, one hundred." I shouted, "Okay, Skee, flash the light around! Hurry!" I struck the match.

There were quick footsteps, which I knew would be Skee dashing into the kitchen. But while I was getting the lamp lit, the screen door to the back porch slammed.

"Hey, Skee," I called, "don't go outside!" I turned up the lamp and put it on the kitchen table, then rushed to the back door. "Hey, Skee! Where are you? Did you see something out there?"

Instead of answering from the yard he came running across the sitting room.

"Where've you been?" I asked, stepping back into the kitchen.

"In the bedroom," he said. "I thought you might need a little more time."

"You mean you weren't even on this side of the house! Who slammed the back door if it wasn't you?"

"Could've been the wind."

"I heard footsteps too!" Just then there was a loud noise in back of us. CLANG! A flour sifter had hit the floor and was rolling across it. I looked at the shelf where it was kept, and there sat Jackson, Miss Julia's cat. "Get down from there!" I said disgustedly. "You know you

:31:

ain't supposed to climb around on shelves."

Jackson hissed at me as if to say he'd climb anywhere he pleased. That cat and I never have been partial to one another. He resents my having free run of the house and looking after it when the women aren't there. He thinks he should be in charge.

"Okay," I said. "So I forgot to feed you tonight! I had other things on my mind." I took a pitcher from the cupboard and poured him a bowl of milk, and he jumped down to drink it. Near his dish there was a big boiler, bottom-side up, that was usually on the shelf.

Skee picked up the boiler. "This must be what you heard earlier. Jackson pushed it down. Maybe he was trying to wake us up to feed him. Cats are smart."

"Jackson's contrary," I said. "Come on, let's go back to bed."

With the cover pulled up, Skee acted as if the thin cotton sheet made us as secure as any fortress could have. "If Jackson knocked down the pans," he said, "and the wind slammed the back door shut, that just about explains everything but the footsteps. Maybe you just thought you heard them."

I wanted so much to believe there'd been no one in the kitchen that I said yes, he was probably right. I wasn't convinced of it, but he was, and soon he was snoring. The katydids and tree frogs set up a racket again but gradually quieted down.

I knew I hadn't just thought I'd heard footsteps, so I got dressed again and took the flashlight and went out to the backyard. I flashed the light all around and then walked out to the chicken house. One of the roosters cackled when I shone the light on him, but nothing else stirred. I walked over to the well shelter next, half expecting something to jump out from behind it. But nothing was there. Finally I went back to bed.

I lay awake. No matter how I tried, I couldn't sleep. The night was so quiet for such a long time that when I heard a loud whistle, I nearly jumped out of bed. It was the freight train that comes through around midnight. If there's anything to be picked up or unloaded at Blyden's Crossing, the train stops. Otherwise it whistles a time or two and keeps right on traveling.

I like trains; they're my link with the outside world. Usually I'm asleep when the freight train passes through, but occasionally I've heard it and the one that passes through at dawn. They reminded me that while I might be snuggled down in bed, the whole world wasn't sleeping. Things were happening—some people were awake and moving around and doing things. And going somewhere. Someday I'd go somewhere too; I'd see lots of places. But tonight the train whistle sounded eerie. I shivered when I heard it again.

5

The Discovery

"Hey! What's the matter!" I yelled, sitting up in bed. I had fallen asleep before dawn, and now the sun was shining brightly. A splash of cold water on my face had wakened me. Skee, already dressed, was standing at the foot of the bed holding a dipper of water.

"I couldn't wake you any other way," he said, looking so happy that I doubted he had tried.

He and Tyler and I used the water method on each other at home sometimes, and it usually led to a fight. It might lead to one now. I got set to jump at him. He could tell what I was about to do, so he threw the rest of the water directly into my face. While I was wiping it out of my eyes and sputtering, he dropped the dipper and ran out, laughing hysterically.

"I'm going home," he yelled back at me.

I put on my clothes and went to the kitchen. Jackson, curled up in a chair near the window, peeked at me and then closed his eyes. He ignored me whenever he could. "I don't like you either," I said cheerfully, "but Miss Julia asked me to feed you." After I'd poured him a bowl of milk I looked for a biscuit to crumble into it. But the bread plate in the cupboard was empty except for a few crumbs. Miss Julia had said she'd leave biscuits for Jackson; it wasn't like her to forget.

I took the milking pail and went to the barn. Mollie mooed softly, as if she were glad to see me. "Okay," I said, "I'll toss you down a little snack." There's plenty of grass in the pasture for her to eat, but she's especially fond of hay. I give her some every now and then as a friendly gesture.

I took the three-prong pitchfork from the feedroom and climbed into the loft. I jabbed the big fork into the hay and nearly keeled over when something jumped up. At first, all I could make out was a blob of white. Then someone shouted, "STOP! STOP!"

My eyes were not used to the dim light, but I could tell either a man or a boy stood in front of me. And he appeared more frightened than I was, perhaps because of the way I held the pitchfork. I'd frozen into position with it in front of me—like a soldier with a bayonet on the end of a rifle, ready to jab the enemy.

"Don't stab me with that thing!" pleaded the intruder.

I made him out to be a boy of around fifteen or sixteen. His voice was deeper than mine, but he wasn't fully grown. He wore faded khaki pants with a white shirt flopped over them. "You're Wilkin Coley!" he said.

"I know who I am!" I said angrily. "Who are you?"

"Can't you see? I'm Alex Folsom. One year I lived near the crossing with my cousins, the Floyds. You know them."

Of course I knew the Floyds. They're the meanest, sorriest folks in our end of the county. Pa says Ol' Damon, the father, should be named Ol' Demon because he's as wicked and cruel as a devil. "You're bigger now," I said.

"Well, I hope so!" said Alex. "That was two years ago."

"What are you doing here?"

"I'm gonna see if the Floyds'll take me back." When I didn't say anything, he added, "They ran me off before."

"You robbed Mr. Larson's store."

"Uncle Damon *said* I robbed it. He wanted an excuse to get rid of me. I was another mouth to feed. I wasn't but thirteen then and couldn't do much work."

"I'm thirteen now," I said, "and I can do a man's work."

"I mean I couldn't find a job for pay or anything, and they were tired of keeping me up."

"Where'd you go?"

"To Atlanta. Ma wasn't too happy to take me back, but she did. And we got along okay till she married again.

: 36 :

Wouldn't you know she'd tie up with a son of a bitch I couldn't get along with!"

I drew back the pitchfork as if I were going to run it through him.

"Hey," he shouted, "don't aim that thing at me!"

I said, "We don't use rough language around here." Then I realized I'd sounded pompous, and I was sorry. Still, Mamma and Pa had drilled it into my brothers and me that if we couldn't say something in plain language without having to swear, then there was something wrong with us instead of with plain language.

"Okay, okay!" said Alex. "But if you'd put down that weapon I'd feel better."

Before I put it down I said, "If you think the Floyds are so no-account, how come you want to go back to them?"

"I gotta be *somewhere*," he said, and I was sorry I'd asked. Of course he had to be somewhere. I reckon I take my home for granted, and here I was acting as if I wouldn't hesitate to ram a pitchfork through him just because he'd slept in the barn. "Come on," I said, tossing a forkful of hay down to Mollie, "I've got to do the milking."

While I went on with the work, he propped himself against the feedroom door, and we talked. In a good light I could tell how much he'd changed since the year he'd spent with the Floyds. Him being older than my brothers and me and living several miles away, we hadn't had much to do with him except that we all rode the school bus together. Some of the girls used to tease each other

: 37 :

about liking him. They'd thought he was the best-looking person they'd ever seen, maybe because he had blond wavy hair and clear skin. The rest of us, boys they'd known all their lives, more often than not had stringy brown hair and freckles. I was sure girls would consider him even more handsome now; they'd probably think they'd found a movie star.

"It was you in the house last night, wasn't it?" I asked.

He explained that it had been him all right. He'd been surprised to hear me and Skee come in, and when he'd realized we were there to spend the night, he decided to wait till we went to sleep and then slip out. But later, when he'd been tipping through the kitchen, he'd knocked over the big boiler. He'd stayed still, thinking we'd heard the noise but would go back to sleep. "I didn't reckon you'd try to sneak up on me," he said.

"You ran out the back door when I yelled for Skee to flash the light around! But how come you didn't go farther than the barn? Seems like anybody who nearly got caught breaking into a house would go farther away than that!"

"Well, I hadn't broken into the house to rob it. I was just wanting a bed for the night."

"Why didn't you go on to the Floyds?"

"To tell the truth, I chickened out. I came down on the afternoon train, bumping around in a boxcar all the way, and the nearer it brought me to Blyden's Crossing the more I dreaded asking the Floyds to take me back."

"I've heard Mrs. Floyd's nice," I said.

"Yeah, Aunt Lettie's all right."

:39:

"Wouldn't she want to help you?"

"It wouldn't matter if she did. They don't pay attention to what she wants. Besides, she made out like she'd been so disappointed in me that I'd nearly been the death of her. I was dreading facing any of 'em, except maybe Young."

Young is the baby of the family; he's a year older than I am. It's his older brothers, Rip and Roger, along with Ol' Damon, who are mean. Young may be as mean, but at least he's not as big.

"Anyway," said Alex, "when I got off the train, the sky was turning so dark it appeared to me the world was coming to an end!"

"It looked that way to me too," I said.

"I've never seen such fierce-looking clouds," said Alex. "And I decided to wait till morning to talk to the Floyds. Late afternoon and night's when they're the meanest."

"They're mean anytime."

"Yeah, I know," he agreed. "But the later in the day it is, the worse they get. I was afraid they'd call the sheriff to come get me, since the robbery never was solved. Or they might've decided to beat me up. When I was living with 'em, I once saw them beat up a man who just happened to be passing along the road. We were sitting on the porch, and Ol' Damon said, 'Go get him!' to Rip and Roger, the way anybody would say 'Sic 'em!' to a dog they wanted to chase after something, and Rip and Roger went tearing out after the man. Them being so much bigger than 'most anybody else, they soon had bloodied that poor man nearly to death."

:40:

"Did the man turn them in?"

"Yeah, but when the sheriff came out there, Ol' Damon said, 'Why, that man was in our smokehouse trying to steal a side of bacon.' And that was the end of it. Ol' Damon made whisky for a crowd that was in with the sheriff. That's how he got by with as much as he did."

I knew about that too. Stories about the whisky crowd go as far back as the hanging of the bootlegger—the one whose ghost I'd seen.

6

Solving a Mystery

Alex followed me to the Todds' house as if I'd invited him to come along. While I strained the milk, he sat down, kicked his feet onto the kitchen table, almost upsetting the sugar dish, and leaned back. "This is a nice place," he said. "When I got off the train yesterday, I saw Miss Julia and Miss Etta up ahead, getting on with suitcases, so I figured their house would be a good place to spend the night. I remembered that folks around here don't lock their doors even when they go on trips. It's different in Atlanta. City folks wouldn't stir from their houses without locking up."

"Did you like living in Atlanta?"

"Yeah, I liked it. It was okay till Ma got married again. Last year I had a job as a bellhop at this hotel, and I was making me some money and having a good time till the night manager went on vacation. The new man found out I wasn't sixteen and fired me, but that hadn't made any difference to the regular one. I could've worked there again after he got back."

Alex talked more about the good job he'd had, and how he'd go back to it eventually, but I was thinking of something else—solving a mystery, maybe. I interrupted him. "Did you come through the woods after you got off the train instead of keeping to the road?" If he'd been coming from Blyden's Crossing at the same time I'd been taking the shortcut from another direction, we would have come out near the house at about the same time. It could've been him I'd seen moving around during the flash of lightning that led me to the hanging tree. Without waiting for him to answer the question, I asked another one. "You weren't just nearly out of the woods when the worst of the storm broke loose, were you?"

"No, of course not!" he said, but he seemed to be holding back a grin. Then he did an imitation that sounded exactly like me: *"I'm coming around there to get you, Ghost! I'm gonna kick you in the tail!"*

I couldn't help laughing. "I didn't say *tail.* I said I'd kick you in the *pants.*"

"Whatever you said, I had to get out of there in a hurry!"

"The back of your shirt looked like a ghost going

: 43 :

through the woods. I nearly fell in an old well giving chase."

"I nearly fell into it getting away!" said Alex. He went over to the cupboard and poured himself a glass of milk. "You don't suppose the ladies would mind if I helped myself to a glass of this, do you?"

I started to ask him what he expected me to do about it if I supposed they would. Maybe he thought I'd get the pitchfork and tell him to leave. "They're big-hearted," I said. "They've never sent anybody away hungry, even bums."

Alex looked hurt, and I added, "Oh, I don't mean that you're a bum, just that whenever anybody asks for a handout, Miss Etta and Miss Julia are always generous."

"Maybe you were right the first time," he said. "Maybe I *am* a bum. Anyway, I'm glad the ladies wouldn't mind that I'm drinking their milk."

"They wouldn't mind that you had some of it last night," I said, and he looked surprised. "And that you ate all the biscuits they'd left for the cat and burned some of their kerosene besides."

"How'd you know?"

"I figured it out."

"There's nothing else in the cupboard," he said, stepping into the pantry. "You don't suppose the ladies would mind if I took a can of something from in here, do you?"

"I suppose they *would*!" I answered.

"How come?" he asked, coming out of the pantry with

a can of sardines and a box of soda crackers. "You said they were generous."

"But they're not here," I reminded him. "It's okay about the milk—and the biscuits. If Jackson don't mind about them, I don't."

At that, Jackson jumped down from the chair where he'd been napping, arched his back, and hissed at Alex. "Anybody Jackson don't like is a true friend of mine!" I said, and we both laughed. Then I became serious again. "Stuff in the cupboard was meant to be used right away, but things in the pantry are provisions for later. It'd be stealing to help yourself. Why don't you buy a can of sardines and some crackers at the store?"

"For the same reason I rode a boxcar yesterday instead of sitting in a comfortable seat—I don't have any money. Even if I did, Mr. Larson's store is the only one nearby, and I ain't wanting to face him first thing."

I pretended to be too busy washing the milking bucket to think about anything else. Out of the corner of my eye I noticed Alex studying the sardine can while Jackson went to his bowl and lapped up the milk I'd poured in it earlier.

"Yeah," Alex said softly, "you're right. I wasn't thinking too clear." He returned to the pantry and came back empty-handed.

I finished the work and was ready to go home. Hungry for my own breakfast, I could sympathize with Alex. "Come eat with us," I suggested. "We don't have a whole lot extra, but Mamma will see that you're fed."

:45:

"No, thanks. There'd be too much explaining to do, and I'd just as soon nobody knew I'm around till I'm squared away with the Floyds and Mr. Larson. You won't tell on me . . . will you?"

We looked at each other, and there was an expression in his eyes that worried me. It reminded me of a stray dog I once found on the far side of our pasture, caught in barbed wire. While I untangled the wire, the dog, completely shackled, had looked at me as if he were not certain whether I planned to help him or hurt him. When he was free, he had bitten me on the ankle and run off.

Alex needed help. Anybody who wanted to move in with the Floyds was desperate. "I won't tell that you're here," I said, and he looked relieved. "And I'll bring you some breakfast—a sausage and biscuit, maybe a couple of 'em. Mamma'll think I've eaten them."

"That'd sure beat facing the Floyds with nothing but a glass of milk in my belly," he said. "Are you sure it won't be too much trouble?"

"No," I said, and then I laughed. "I'd rather contend with you than a ghost!" He laughed too, and when I started away I called back to him. "An idea is shaping up in my head. I may figure out a way to keep you from having to go back to the Floyds."

7
"Rescue the Perishing"

Pauline, the first calf that Miss Etta and Miss Julia had given my brothers and me, was now a grown cow with a calf of her own. She was giving more milk than the calf or we could use. At breakfast Skee said, "Maybe we ought to sell the extra milk and make us lots of money."

Pa laughed. "Nobody makes *lots* of money nowadays."

Mamma said, "Maybe you boys should sell Pauline and make a *little* money."

"What?" all three of us said at the same time, and Skee added, "Pauline's like a sister to me!"

"Or an aunt," said Tyler.

Pa said, "I've always looked on her more like a cousin."

:47:

"Now be serious, all of you!" said Mamma. "Maybe the extra milk could be sold, but one of you would have to deliver it. And milking an extra cow already puts too much work on Tyler. It's all right now, but when school starts, he'd have to get up before daylight to do everything." I said that maybe I could milk Pauline, but Mamma said then I'd have to get up before daylight. Skee volunteered for the job too, but the rest of us agreed that he wasn't big enough to handle such a task yet; maybe in another year.

We didn't solve the problem while we were eating, but I was glad that we had something to talk about. Everybody concentrated on it instead of noticing that I slipped a sausage and a biscuit into my pocket. A few minutes later I took another of each. Then Pa mapped out the jobs he wanted us to do during the day. "Without fail!" he added as he left for his job at the sawmill, which meant we'd better have the work done before he returned home. Sometimes when he told us about things he wanted done we knew we could take our time. But "without fail" meant *Today!*

My main assignment was to hoe out the pole beans. But before going to work I would take Alex his breakfast. "I'm going back up to the Todds'," I said, trying to sound casual.

"How come?" asked Tyler.

"To put Mollie in the pasture. I forgot to let her out of the barn."

"I'll let her out," said Tyler, "I'm gonna take the shortcut," which meant he would pass the barn on his way to

Mr. Madden's. He was to return a plowshaft we had borrowed.

"I thought you didn't like to take the shortcut."

"I don't like it during a storm," said Tyler.

As he started out, I called, "I might have let Mollie out. Just doublecheck as you go past." I knew full well that I had put her in the pasture.

At the toolshed I picked up a hoe. I planned to sneak away from the pole beans long enough to take the food to Alex, but Skee followed me to the garden. He was to weed the strawberries. Usually he has to be reminded of a job several times before he gets around to it.

After I'd hit a few licks with the hoe, I said, "I've got to run up to the Todds' for a minute, but I'll be right back."

"What're you going for?"

"I forgot to give Jackson some fresh milk."

"I'll go with you," said Skee, dropping a handful of weeds at the end of the row.

"You'd better finish the berries."

"I'll finish 'em when you get back to the beans."

"I suddenly remember something," I said.

"What?"

"That I didn't settle with you for pouring cold water in my face!"

Skee's quick, and he knows when to start running. He lit out before I'd finished the sentence, and he wasn't about to follow me now. I hurried to the Todds'.

I expected to find Alex in the kitchen, but he wasn't there. "Anybody home?" I called, walking through the

:49:

front part of the house. "Where are you, Alex?" There was no answer.

Back in the kitchen I put the sausage and biscuits on the table. Jackson eyed them, so I moved them to the cupboard.

I heard a loud whistle and knew that it was the morning passenger train. Maybe Alex was stealing onto a boxcar and heading back to Atlanta. I looked at Jackson. "If Alex is not here tonight, you get the sausage and biscuits." Instead of appearing pleased, Jackson hissed, so I added, "On the other hand, I may eat them myself."

Somehow I felt that Alex was gone for good. On the way home I wondered if I'd ever know what became of him.

I had a feeling that Alex was all right, wherever he was. It was hard to imagine that anything could go wrong on a day like this. The sun was shining, and red clover, refreshed by yesterday's rain, bloomed along the path. In the distance I could hear the call of a bobwhite, always a pleasant sound. A yellow butterfly, as if it were leading the way, flew just ahead of me. I was watching it and listening to the bobwhite when "YEEOOW!" I was scared nearly out of my senses. Alex had jumped out at me from behind a thicket of briers, screaming shrilly. He laughed uproariously. "Scared you, didn't I?"

"Not a bit," I said disgustedly. "What're you doing out here?"

"Picking some blackberries." He went behind the briers and brought out a small pan that he'd borrowed from the kitchen. It was half-filled with berries. "I thought I'd have a dish of 'em with some milk and sugar. You don't suppose the ladies would mind if I took a spoonful or two of sugar, do you?" Before I could answer he added, "I know. They're kind and generous."

"Well, they are," I said, as if he'd been making fun of me or Miss Etta and Miss Julia.

When he realized I was mad, he stopped laughing. He slapped me on the back and said, "I was picking enough for you too, Cowboy! Come on, let's go have a bowlful."

"I've got work to do."

"When I get settled down," said Alex, "I'll pay the ladies back for anything I've taken, I promise you. In the meantime, if you think I ought not to borrow even one spoon of sugar, then I won't. I promise."

I was back to feeling friendly toward him. "They'd want you to help yourself. In fact, I was wondering how you'd like to stay with them instead of with the Floyds."

"Are you crazy? I don't have any money to pay for room and board."

"Maybe they'd let you work for it. I do their milking and wood-hauling and things like that, but we've got more than enough work to do at home. The Todd Sisters might give you a room and meals in exchange for some work around the place. You'd be sort of a hired man, but they'd treat you more like you were kin to them. They're—" I paused, then Alex and I added at the same time, "kind and generous!" We both laughed.

"They're coming back tomorrow. I'll ask 'em if they won't let you stay with them."

"I could sure help 'em out," said Alex. "Only one problem: I don't know how to milk."

"I could teach you."

"I can haul wood and do whatever else they want done. I got some faults, I know, but laziness ain't one of 'em."

"Good," I said, "because it occurs to me that you could work for Mr. Larson too."

"Now hold on! What are you, a job agency?"

"Well, you're in trouble with Mr. Larson, right?"

"Right."

"Then work off whatever debt he feels you owe him. It'd beat going to jail."

"What wouldn't? But do you think he'd want me around?"

"He's all the time needing somebody to help move stuff from one place to another or haul out trash and clean up the store. He hires me every now and then, but if he had you to come in once or twice a week—maybe just on Saturdays when school starts—he'd feel better toward you."

"He might or he might not," said Alex. "I remember that Mr. Larson's mean."

"No," I said, "he's not mean. He's stern, but he's fair."

Tyler and Skee might agree with Alex; they think Mr. Larson's cross and cantankerous. They insist that I do the talking whenever we trade eggs for groceries, and I usually hold out for a fair bargain. I admit that talking with him is not always pleasant, but I didn't say so to

Alex. I added in a boastful tone, "I get along very well with Mr. Larson."

Alex was quiet a moment, then he said, "I don't suppose you'd speak to him about me? If I went to the store he might have me locked up before he'd heard my offer. It might help if somebody sort of discussed it with him first."

After bragging about how well I got along with Mr. Larson, I hated to say that I didn't relish the idea of talking with him about Alex. I remembered how mad Mr. Larson had been when Alex ran away before anything was settled about the robbery. Still, I knew that Alex needed somebody to talk to Mr. Larson for him, and if I wasn't willing to help him I doubted that anybody would. It somehow seemed my moral duty. Recently we had talked in Sunday School about people who claim to be so upright and good when they're at church but who don't live up to their religion during the rest of the week.

"I'll do it," I promised. "I'll help you out." Proud of my noble intentions, I walked away whistling the hymn "Rescue the Perishing." Remembering the pole beans, I told myself not to feel too good. If I didn't get the work done by the time Pa came home, somebody would need to rescue me.

: 55 :

8

A Bargain

It was so hot in midafternoon that it would have been a good idea to rest in the shade every now and then. But I was in a hurry to finish hoeing out the beans. I wanted to go to the store, and I knew better than to take off before the work was done. Pa and I get along fine, and one reason is that I do what I'm told. And I'd been told to hoe out the beans. Pa doesn't like to whip any of us, but he never hesitates from doing what he calls his "bounding duty" when we fail to mind him.

Skee came back to his job of weeding the strawberries, but he did more talking than weeding.

"I'm busy, even if you're not," I told him. He didn't

have to concentrate on doing a good job the way I did. Skee being the littlest, Pa lets him get by with sloppy work that wouldn't be tolerated from me or Tyler.

After a while Big Will came by to tell us that Mr. Madden planned to pick squash the next afternoon. We agreed to be in the field by 12:30, and Big Will started away.

"Stay on and let's sing," said Skee. "I heard a new song on the radio. It's called 'Red Sails in the Sunset.'"

"How does it go?" asked Big Will.

Skee was happy to sing it for him, and after listening to the words only once, Big Will joined in. Nobody made me stop to listen, but I leaned on my hoe and enjoyed the brief concert. Big Will's got a fine voice, and Skee does all right too. He can sing a whole lot better than he can weed strawberries, that's for sure. After Big Will left, Skee pulled a few more weeds and announced that he was finished.

"You are not!"

"Yes, I am. And I'm going to the house." He started away.

"You come back here and do the job right!" I called, knowing that tomorrow I'd probably have to weed the strawberries he had missed. Just then I heard, "Psst! Psst! Let him go!" I looked around.

"I'm over here behind this row of corn." It was Alex. "As soon as your brother's farther away I'll come out."

I stepped over to where Alex was waiting. He asked, "Are you gonna talk to Mr. Larson for me?"

"Sure," I said. "I promised, didn't I? Only I've got work to do first."

"I'll help you. Have you got another hoe?"

"Yeah, but if I went to the house to get it somebody'd want to know why."

"Then I'll work while you go to the store," he said, taking the hoe from me. "While you're doing something for me, I'll do something for you." He smiled. "That's a fair trade, ain't it, Cowboy?" Instead of waiting for an answer, he started hoeing. I didn't have to tell him how to do the job. He worked fast, and he didn't miss a sprig of grass or a weed.

I stood at the end of the garden, and when I saw Skee coming back along the path, I called to Alex, "Get behind the corn, quick!" I grabbed the hoe and went to work, pretending not to notice Skee till he was right at me. He had left his baseball cap alongside a row of berries, but he couldn't remember which row. In order to get rid of him, I helped him find the cap. When Skee left, Alex came out again. He took over my job, and I went to the store.

The only other customer when I arrived was Young Floyd, Alex's sorry cousin. He was looking at the pocketknives in the small showcase where special items were displayed. Mr. Larson had said last spring that some new knives were on order. Tyler would be glad to hear they had finally arrived; he had been saving his money to buy one.

"Howdy-do, Wilkin?" said Young. "Been winning any

prizes at school lately?" He was being sarcastic. He never missed a chance to remind me that one year I had beaten everybody in grammar school in spelling matches, math drills, and in contests in other subjects as well. Young always acted as if it should have been an embarrassment to me.

"There's no school in summer," I said. "Didn't you know that?"

"Ain't none for me no time now," he said. "I don't have to go no more."

"How come? You're not sixteen."

"Rip and Roger whipped the truant officer the last time he came to check on me, and he ain't bothered to come around no more. So I ain't gonna fool with school again."

I could have told him that he didn't learn anything when he did fool with it. But he was so much bigger than I that I decided not to stick that close to the facts.

"Why don't you buy me a belly washer and a candy bar?" he asked, with a smile that looked more like a snarl. "Just to be neighborly." He had cornered Skee in the store not long ago and made him spend a quarter, all the spending money Skee'd had in a long time.

"I ain't as neighborly as Skee," I said, letting him know that I knew what he'd done. "Besides, I don't have any money."

"I know you have so," he said angrily. "You make it working for Mr. Madden. I'll just see if you've got any." He grabbed me around the neck and rammed his hand in my overalls' pocket. I tried to squirm free, but it was like trying to get loose from a lion. Usually I'm on guard when I'm around him, but I hadn't expected him to jump me in the store. He had a stranglehold on me.

Suddenly I heard *Whack!* and Young let me go. Mr. Larson had struck him with a thick yardstick. "Don't ever bother one of my customers again, Young Floyd!" said Mr. Larson. "Do you hear!"

Mr. Larson's a big man, but Young's nearly as big. He looked at Mr. Larson sullenly and then said, "I'll do what I please."

"Clear out of here," said Mr. Larson. "Now get!" He drew back the yardstick as if he were going to strike Young again.

"I'm going," said Young, and under his breath he whispered to me, "I'll get you!"

When Young was out of the way, Mr. Larson asked, "What can I do for you, Wilkin?" He appeared so riled up still that I knew this was no time to mention Alex. He asked me again, "What can I do for you?"

"Oh, I'm not trading this time, Mr. Larson. There was something I wanted to ask you, but maybe I'd better come back another time."

"Out with it!" said Mr. Larson. "What's wrong?" I almost feared he'd take the yardstick to me if I didn't tell him.

"Nothing's wrong, Mr. Larson. That is, I was just wondering . . . if . . . er . . . if you remember Alex Folsom."

"Alex Folsom!" He shouted it. "He's as sorry as his Floyd kin. You know he left here after breaking into my

: 61 :

store, don't you? I ought to've had him brought back and tried. I'll still do it if he ever sets foot in these parts."

"It could be that some of the Floyds broke in the store and then laid it on him."

"He owes me a debt," said Mr. Larson grumpily.

"I was wondering if maybe you'd let him work off his debt to you."

"I wouldn't want him in my sight."

"Maybe he's reformed by now. Don't you believe in giving anybody a second chance?"

"What's all this about?" he asked crossly, and I told him I'd heard that Alex wanted to come back to Blyden's Crossing. "He's grown up a lot since he was here," I said, "and if you want to give him a part-time job instead of trying to send him to jail, it would be a righteous deed." Mr. Larson is the superintendent of our Sunday School, so I threw in some quotations from the Bible about turning the other cheek and things like that. I rattled on as fast as I could, and gradually Mr. Larson didn't seem so mad. Maybe I just wore him down.

Finally he asked, "Would you stand back of him?"

"Come again," I said, meaning I didn't understand.

"Are you willing to promise me that he'll behave himself?"

"Oh, yes, sir."

"And in the event he doesn't, you'll be responsible to me. In effect, you're going on his bond. If he fails me or steals anything, you're to make up for it, all right?"

I thought about it for a minute. In trading eggs for groceries, I'd faced Mr. Larson at least once a week, bargaining with him. Once I'd threatened to take the eggs to a store in town if he didn't allow a better price for them. I hadn't figured on making any sort of bargain with him today.

"Well, are you?" he asked. "Are you willing to accept those terms?"

I was too deep into this to back down now. "Yes, sir," I said, looking Mr. Larson square in the eyes. "Yes, I'll accept 'em."

"Then I guess I could give Alex a chance," he said. "You can get that word to him."

"I will," I said, hurrying out. "And thank you. Thank you a lot, Mr. Larson."

On the way home I watched for Young Floyd. It'd be just like him to be hiding somewhere, waiting to pick a fight. But he was nowhere around.

When I returned to the garden, Alex had disappeared. So had the hoe. And the work wasn't near finished. In fact, almost nothing had been done while I was gone.

There was no way I could finish the beans before it was time to get on with the milking chores. I'd be in for a bad night when Pa got home, and Alex was to blame. I was disgusted with him for not living up to his part of our bargain and was almost mad enough to race back to the store and tell Mr. Larson, "No, I won't stand bond for Alex!"

Of course, there was a chance that Pa would be too tired to go out and look at the garden, but that was doubtful. He told us once, "Nothing uplifts my weary ol' soul more than watching things grow, whether it's you boys or the plants you tend in the garden." I knew that with the back-breaking work he did at the sawmill he needed something to uplift his soul, and I was ashamed that I'd let him down. Knowing that he'd take his belt to me didn't make me feel any better.

9

The Warning of the Screech Owl

After I'd finished the milking chores at the Todds', I fed the half-grown pigs that always wanted more ears of corn than I shucked for them. "There'd be nothing left for tomorrow," I told the shoats, "if you ate everything now." They acted as if they'd just as soon be given their lifetime supply of food immediately. The chickens were nearly as greedy. They pecked the corn that I shelled for them as fast as the kernels hit the ground. Next, I drew water and took a bucketful to the shoats. Then I drew more and divided it between the chickens and Mollie's calf. Mollie had access to the stream in the pasture and could drink from it. Then I hurried home. Pa might take it easy on me if I was at work when he got there.

But I was too late. He was coming from the garden as I was heading toward it. We greeted each other, and he put one arm around my shoulders while we walked to the house. At the back porch I said, "I'd just as soon have it now."

He looked puzzled. "Have what?"

"My punishment for not getting the beans done right."

"They looked fine to me," he said. "It was so hot today that I was afraid I'd given you too much work. I'm proud of the way you did it. Yes, sir, you did a bang-up job." He started into the house, but I lingered on the porch. As soon as he was inside, I ran to the garden.

I couldn't believe it: The beans had been hoed as clean as if I'd worked all day in them. I stood there, believing in miracles, till Alex stepped out from behind a thicket of plum bushes. He leaned on the hoe. "I've never been as tired in my life!" he said.

"You finished the beans!"

"I promised you, didn't I?"

I laughed; there was no sense in being mad at him now. He must have returned to work just after I'd gone to do the milking. He said that earlier he had walked into the woods to cool off but had stayed longer than he'd planned.

"Say," he said, "while I was in the woods, I came onto the stream. There's a dandy spot for a small pond. In fact, I pulled in a little mud with the hoe to start a dam, but if you and your brothers would help me, we could

: 66 :

take shovels and really move in some dirt."

"We tried it one year," I said, "but the first big rain washed the dam away."

"That'd be okay," he said. "We'd have us a place to swim till the first big rain!"

Just then I heard Mamma ringing the bell that she uses to call us to meals, so I started away. I was sorry that Alex couldn't come along; he must have been starved.

"Will you be in the barn tonight?" I asked.

"Yeah, I guess."

"Then I'll see that you have something to eat at bedtime. Skee and Tyler'll be spending the night up there with me, but I'll slip off from them some way."

During supper, Skee said, "Reckon the ghost'll be moving around tonight?"

"I'm not afraid of a ghost," I said.

"You were last night."

"That was last night. I decided today that it's foolish to believe in such things."

Mamma said, "Now you're being reasonable."

"How reasonable do you suppose he is?" asked Tyler as if he were talking to everybody but me. "Reckon he'd spend the night up there by himself?"

"Sure I would!" I bragged. I hadn't thought of it earlier, but if I went by myself then Alex could stay in the house instead of having to sleep in the barn. And the family would think I was being brave, spending the night in the house alone.

"I'll bet you won't!" said Tyler.

"I'll bet I will."

"No," said Mamma. "I think Tyler or Skee should go with you."

Pa spoke up. "Let the boy try it by himself if he wants to. We menfolks have to prove things to ourselves from time to time. Maybe Wilkin wants to convince himself that he's not afraid of ghosts."

By then we'd finished supper, and I had not put anything into my pockets for Alex. I didn't even think about it until I heard Tyler asking about a piece of meatloaf and two biscuits. It was his turn to help clear the table, and he wanted to know if the leftovers should be put in the cupboard.

"No," said Mamma. "There's not enough to warm over. Give them to Ally Greevy."

"I'll take them to him," I said, snatching the plate away from Tyler.

In the yard Ally Greevy, who'd been fed earlier in the day, wagged his tail excitedly. "Go catch yourself a rabbit!" I said, putting the meatloaf and biscuits into a piece of newspaper. I hid the package in the fork of a pecan tree, out of Ally Greevy's reach. He barked at it as if he had treed a cat or a possum.

At bedtime I took the package with me. I also took along a flashlight, but the light it gave off was so weak it wasn't much help. By the time I reached the barn, the batteries were dead.

"Alex?" I called. "Are you there?"

"Yeah," he answered from the loft. "That you, Wilkin?"

I lowered my voice. "No, it's the sheriff come to get you!" It was a bad joke, but he laughed. "I've got you something to eat," I said. "And you can come spend the night in the house. I'm by myself."

"Good!" he said, striking a match. He did not look like himself in the eerie light. Even his shadow, from where I stood beneath him, was distorted. It looked ten feet long and appeared to float across the rafters.

"Careful of the match," I warned, "with all that hay around!"

He blew out the light and climbed down the ladder, feeling his way in the dark. More familiar with the barn than he was, I led him outside, and we started toward the house. He held on to one of my overall straps in order to stay on the path. The night was so dark and silent that I was glad someone was close by, especially when we went near the hanging tree. Suddenly there was a screeching noise from high up in it.

"God A'mighty!" said Alex. "What was that?"

"A screech owl."

"That's supposed to be a sign of bad luck, ain't it?"

"It's a sign of death," I said.

"Whose death?"

"Yours or mine, I suppose. I don't imagine anybody else heard the screeching."

"I'm not superstitious," he said, and I told him I wasn't either but that lots of folks were. Some of them think that if a screech owl is heard in the night the only way to ward off danger is to tie a knot in the corner of a bed sheet. According to the belief, that'll choke the owl.

In the house I found the big lamp and lit it, and we made our way to the back bedroom. We talked for a few minutes, him telling me about Atlanta and the job he'd had at the hotel, but soon both of us went to sleep.

I slept soundly and might not have wakened at daybreak if Alex hadn't been coughing so loud that no one could possibly have stayed asleep. He coughed for a long time.

"Are you sick?" I asked.

"No," he sputtered, continuing to cough. When he let up, he turned over and was quiet. I don't know why the screech owl crossed my mind as I was getting dressed, but it did.

I let the chickens out of the hen house, fed the shoats, and did the milking. When I returned to the house to strain the milk, Alex was coughing again. Maybe he'd caught a cold the afternoon he'd been out in the storm. Or possibly he'd gotten too hot working so fast in the garden yesterday.

I went home, and at breakfast Pa told Tyler, Skee, and me that we could have the morning to do as we pleased. There were no special jobs, and we could save our strength to help Mr. Madden with the squash in the afternoon. While Pa was talking I put bacon strips and two biscuits into my back pockets. Next I unfastened the bib pocket of my overalls and tried to slide a fried egg into it. I held the platter of eggs over my plate as if I were serving myself to an extra one.

"Goodness!" said Mamma. "What on earth have you done?"

Half of the egg was inside the pocket. The other half flopped over the outside. Tyler and Skee laughed.

"It slid off the platter," I said, taking the egg and holding it out as if it were a turtle that might snap at me.

Pa smiled. "If you'd been trying to put an egg in your pocket, it never would have landed there!"

I realized that everyone thought it had been an accident, so I laughed too. Mamma said, "Put the egg back on the plate. We'll let Ally Greevy have it."

After breakfast I went back to the Todds', being careful to slip off without Tyler or Skee.

"Wake up!" I called to Alex. "Miss Etta and Miss Julia'll be coming in on the morning train, and you'd better be out of here." He didn't say anything, and I called louder, "Wake up, Alex! Wake up!"

He still didn't answer, so I put my hands on his shoulders and shook him. He was as warm as Skee had been the time he'd had diphtheria. "You're feverish," I said, when Alex was finally awake. "But you'd better get up."

He stumbled out, and while he dressed I made up the bed so the ladies would find everything orderly. I untied the knot in the corner of the sheet on his side of the bed and didn't have the heart to tease him about being superstitious.

As we started through the kitchen I offered Alex the bacon and biscuits, but he said, "I don't want anything to eat."

"It's your breakfast," I insisted. I'd never heard of anybody not wanting breakfast.

"Give it to the cat," he said, swatting at Jackson who

was staring at us from a chair by the door.

"You better come home with me. You're sick," I said, starting from the house.

Alex followed me. "I'm okay. I'll sleep in the barn awhile; then I'll be all right." He sounded as if he were in a daze, and he looked weary.

In the barn he fell backwards when he tried to climb the ladder. I pulled him to his feet and steadied him as he started up the ladder again. He was so shaky that I climbed up too, staying just back of him in case he fell again. I waited until he was settled in the hay; then I left.

"I'll talk to the ladies," I called back to him. "I'll meet the train and tote their suitcases home. On the way I'll ask 'em about taking you in."

"Thanks, Cowboy," he answered weakly.

10

Close Call

"Why, sure, we'll give the boy a home," said Miss Julia.

But Miss Etta was not certain that it was a good idea. "Remember Rudie!" she said. Rudie had been a squirrel I'd found when he was so young his eyes weren't open. He had fallen from a nest high in the hanging tree, and his parents had refused to take him back. Miss Julia had looked after him so well that it wasn't long before he was running everywhere. He had stayed outdoors most of the time, but he had free run of the house too. He became everyone's pet; even Jackson had loved him. Then one day Rudie had turned on Miss Julia and bitten her hand.

Afterwards she came down with blood poisoning and almost died.

"I'm not going to let a bad experience with a squirrel keep me from helping the homeless," argued Miss Julia.

"But it sounds as if the boy has a home," said Miss Etta. "It's just that he can't get along with his stepfather. Sooner or later he'll have to learn that few arrangements in life are perfect."

We were talking as we walked home from the depot at Blyden's Crossing. I had planned to carry their suitcases, but Miss Etta insisted on carrying her own. Miss Julia and I carried the other one, swinging it between us.

By the time we got to their house, Miss Etta had agreed that they would talk with Alex. I hurried to the barn to tell him, but I couldn't wake him. I shouted; I shook him; I even took the bucket of water from the calf's stall and splashed some of it on him. He groaned and rolled over.

Miss Etta came out to see what was taking so long. "I'll have a look," she said, starting up the ladder.

"Careful you don't fall!" I warned.

"Don't forget, young man," she said, "I did the milking and looked after the stock here before you did. I'm perfectly capable of climbing to the loft." By the time she finished saying it, she had done it.

Kneeling alongside Alex, she felt his forehead. "Goodness!" she said. "He has a high fever." She dampened her handkerchief in the calf's bucket and put it on Alex's forehead, ordering me to fetch fresh water from the well. "And holler for Julia to give you a towel."

In a few minutes I returned with water and a towel. Miss Julia came out to the barn too, but she didn't climb to the loft. She's not as strong as Miss Etta.

Miss Etta sponged off Alex's head and chest with the cool water, and finally he roused enough for us to help him from the loft. Then, by supporting him on each side, we got him to the house and into bed.

"I'll make some herb tea for him," said Miss Julia.

And Miss Etta said, "Wilkin, you get him undressed while I look for something to put on him."

While I was getting Alex out of his clothes, he mumbled, "Don't beat me! I'll give it back! I'll give it back!" He said more, but I couldn't understand him.

"He's out of his head," said Miss Etta, handing me a nightgown that must have been way too big for her or Miss Julia. It fit Alex fine, but if he wasn't sick already he would have become ill as soon as he saw the lace on the sleeves and the pink roses stitched around the collar.

Miss Julia came into the room, and Miss Etta asked, "Have you ever nursed a sick boy?" Miss Julia helps neighbors when they need someone who knows about nursing chores.

"No, I haven't," said Miss Julia, turning to me. "Your mamma's had more experience in doctoring boys than we have, Wilkin. Suppose you run home and ask her if she'll come give us a hand."

Of course Mamma was willing to go to their aid, but she insisted that I stay at home and keep the fire going in the kitchen stove. In addition to the vegetables she was cooking for our lunch, she was making strawberry jam. She told me to keep chunks of wood burning in the fire box and every now and then stir the jam.

By the time I had added wood to the fire the second time, Mamma was back. "Etta wants you to go into town and ask Dr. Sanders to come out here," she said. I started away, and Mamma called, "If you should see Mr. Hurd heading back to town, ask him if he'll give the message to Dr. Sanders, and you come back home." Mr. Hurd is our mailman.

Before I got to Blyden's Crossing I saw Young Floyd on the road coming toward me. I started to duck into the woods till he went past, but then I'd lose time. Besides, I wasn't going to let him bully me into being afraid to move about the countryside. So I walked ahead, mustering strength by telling myself that I might not be as big as he was but that I was tough. "Tough as steel!" I said, lowering my head and walking as straight toward him as if I were a torpedo on a deadly course.

"Well, howdy-do?" said Young, stopping on the side of the road and smiling his snarly smile.

"I do very well," I said, not missing a step in my torpedo stride, "but I don't have time to discuss it now. I'm on my way to get Dr. Sanders."

He didn't ask who was sick. Instead he called after me, "I ain't forgot that you didn't buy me no belly washer yesterday. I'll get even."

"I haven't forgot a lot of things," I called back. I was far enough away so that if he wanted to fight he'd have to race me to town.

Soon Mr. Hurd came along. He stopped to offer me a ride, and I explained that Dr. Sanders was needed at the Todds'. "I'll be going by the doctor's house in a few minutes," said Mr. Hurd. "I'll make sure he gets the message."

By the time I returned home, Tyler and Skee were having lunch. Skee said, "You'd better eat in a hurry. It's time to go pick squash."

"Mr. Madden'll wait for us," I said. "Where's Mamma?"

"She's gone back to the Todds'," said Tyler, passing me a bowl of butterbeans and a plate of biscuits. Skee pushed a dish of mashed potatoes toward me. While we were eating they wanted to hear all about Alex and how I'd kept it a secret that he was back. "Wilkin's Ghost," Skee called him.

Alex had pneumonia, and for a week we weren't sure whether he was going to live or die. Mamma spent a lot of time helping the Todd Sisters look after him, and Dr. Sanders came every day.

Finally Alex started getting better, and Tyler, Skee, and I were allowed to visit him. Whenever we didn't have chores to do we'd go to the Todds'. One afternoon when we arrived, Miss Julia was reading aloud to Alex. "I'll quit and let you boys visit," she said, but we insisted that she keep reading. The book was *The Call of the Wild*, and it was fun to hear a little delicate woman like Miss Julia reading such lines as, "Some dam fine day heem get mad lak hell an' den heem chew dat Spitz all up an' spit

: 78 :

heem out on de snow," as if she were one of the characters talking about the sled dogs. She read till Alex asked if it wasn't time for some refreshments.

Miss Julia laughed. "Why, yes, I suppose it is. I'll make a pitcher of lemonade."

For us, refreshments are rare and special, and while Miss Julia was out of the room Skee said, "That was a real good idea, Alex! I never would have thought about telling Miss Julia that we ought to have something good to drink!"

Tyler said, "No, and don't you ever think of it! It's not for us to suggest such things."

Alex said, "They like to wait on me." Then he did an imitation of Miss Etta and Miss Julia talking, sounding just like them. In his imitation Miss Etta scolded Miss Julia: *"You're spoiling the boy, cooking everything you think he'll like and more besides."* Then, sounding like Miss Julia, he said, *"Well, you're one to talk! Ordering him pants and shoes from Sears Roebuck."* Then it was Miss Etta again: *"Who made the pajamas? And who's making all the new shirts?"*

He stopped when Miss Julia called, "Etta? Is that you, Etta?" She came into the bedroom, bringing a big tray. "I thought I heard Etta. I could have sworn I did. I thought maybe she'd gotten home early."

"No, she's not home yet," said Alex, while Miss Julia stirred the lemonade. She served all of us a glass of it and some tea cakes she'd made that morning.

It didn't take long for word to get around that Alex was back. At the store one day Mr. Larson told me that

: 80 :

he planned to live up to our bargain whenever Alex was ready to go to work. "That is, if you still have faith in him," said Mr. Larson.

"Yes, sir, I have faith in him."

"I'm sure you've heard the story that's going around," he added.

"What story?"

"That the boy was run off from home by his stepfather for stealing a watch. That's what Damon Floyd's telling, and he's the boy's uncle."

"He's just mad 'cause Alex can get along without him," I said. It was like Ol' Damon to circulate a vicious rumor. He'd probably have it in for me too for helping Alex.

I stopped by to chat with Alex on the way home. Both the ladies were there, and Alex said, "I'm glad to see you, Wilkin. I've decided to put on my clothes and start learning the chores. I'll go with you when it's time to milk."

Miss Julia said, "Maybe you'd better stay in for a few more days."

Miss Etta didn't agree. "Get up, Alex, if you'd like," she said. "Julia's having such a good time playing nurse that she'll turn you into an invalid if you let her."

All of us laughed, including Miss Julia, and I was certain that everything was going to work out fine. I could tell that the Todd Sisters, after nursing Alex back to health, wouldn't want him to go away. Like Rudie, the squirrel, he was their pet.

: 81 :

11

A Ringing in the Rails

Soon Alex was back to full strength, and I went with him to talk to Mr. Larson. It was agreed that "the debt," as Mr. Larson called it, would be paid if Alex worked all day Saturdays and three afternoons a week for two months. I thought it was too much, Alex having been falsely accused in the first place, but Alex agreed to it.

Mr. Larson handed him the broom and told him he could start by sweeping out the store. "Or maybe you'd better take that trash out first," he said, pointing toward a pile of empty boxes.

Alex took an armload of boxes outside. I started to follow him, but Mr. Larson stopped me. He wanted to remind me that this whole idea had been mine; it was clear that he still didn't have faith in it. He believed Ol' Damon's lies about Alex's stepfather chasing him out of Atlanta. "I don't trust the boy," said Mr. Larson, "but I'm not going back on my word."

Everyone else got off to a better start with Alex—even the animals at the Todds'. Jackson was a bit slow in warming up to him, but the livestock took to him immediately. He could shuck and shell corn faster than I could, and he was generous with it. The chickens preferred him to me. And the shoats liked anyone who fed them, so they squealed their approval whenever Alex was near. Even Mollie was contented. It would have been a tribute to me if she had kicked him a time or two, but she didn't act as if she realized there'd been a change. "Now, now, Mollie!" Alex would say. "Don't be nervous! It's just ol' Alex squeezing away down here with one hand at a time." Soon he was milking with both hands and finishing the job quicker than I ever had. Everything he undertook he did well—and fast.

On the days Mr. Madden needed help, Alex went with us unless he had to be at the store. He could pick squash faster than anybody but Big Will. And he could wash and grade the vegetables in such a hurry that Mr. Madden wasn't sure the job was being done right. When he discovered that no mistakes had been made, he said he'd rather have Alex on the job than one of those new grading machines he'd been wishing he could afford.

The squash soon played out, and the beans weren't ready, so we had some time off in midsummer. We probably wouldn't have done anything special if Alex hadn't wanted to build a pond.

There was a place along the stream where the high banks on each side widened out to form a small pool. At the end of it, where the banks grew close together, we'd pile rocks and mud in the gap to form a small dam. The dam then held back the water in the slow-moving stream, and the pool became deep enough for swimming —till a heavy rain washed part or all of our dam away. But we didn't have anything more urgent to do and would get busy and build it back.

One hot day I was longing for a swim, but we had to stay home and help Mamma make soup mixture. She cans lots of it for winter use, and on days when she makes a batch she keeps all of us busy. In addition to gathering the vegetables, we have to get them ready to go into the pot. This means shucking and silking corn and cutting it off the cob, shelling butterbeans till our fingers are practically nubs, peeling tomatoes, and slicing okra.

Around three o'clock Alex came along to see if we wanted to go swimming, but we were still busy. He helped us finish the work, and then we started to the woods. When we were almost out of earshot of the house, Mamma called that one of us must go to the store for her. I knew it was my turn, but I argued with Tyler and Skee about it. They kept walking toward the woods, and I had to go back to the house. Mamma needed baking powder, she said, before she could make biscuits for supper.

I dreaded going to the store. Alex had been working there for three weeks, and Mr. Larson would have saved up all sorts of complaints for me. "Couldn't you make biscuits without baking powder?" I asked.

Mamma laughed. "They'd be little flat rocks!"

"But it may rain tonight," I protested. Mamma said nothing. "And the dam'll wash away. And we won't have a good swimming place, maybe not ever as good as it is now."

"If you'd hurry," said Mamma, "you might get back in time for a swim." The way she said it I knew she wouldn't change her mind, so I went ahead to the store.

Ol' Tom Berle was sitting on a bench out front when I went inside, and Mr. Waldrup was coming out with a horse collar and a bag of groceries. Nobody was in the back but Mr. Larson, and I expected him to start complaining the minute he saw me. Instead, he came out from behind the counter and shook my hand as if I were some visitor from far off. Then he started bragging on Alex. "Why, that boy's got this place shined up cleaner than it's been in years!" I looked around the store and could tell a difference all right. Merchandise had been straightened up, and the shelves had been painted. "It was Alex's idea," said Mr. Larson. "In a day or two he's gonna get started painting the walls." He sounded as if he'd never have thought of putting a coat of paint on anything if Alex hadn't suggested it. "And he's gonna letter a sign to go out front." He talked on about all the plans he and Alex had for the store. Then he said, "I think you're right."

"About what?"

"That maybe Ol' Damon just made up that story about

Alex's stepfather running him off. Why, he's a good boy!"

I was so surprised by Mr. Larson's enthusiasm that I forgot to buy the baking powder. Halfway home I remembered it and hurried back to the store. On the way out the second time, I heard the whistle of the afternoon train. I knew it was too late to get in a swim before time to do the late-afternoon chores, so I decided to go down to the depot. I never tired of seeing the train pull in.

It got there just as I did. Nobody was waiting alongside the tracks to board it, but that's not unusual. There are never many passengers at the crossing.

When the train stopped, the conductor hopped to the ground. A porter handed down a satchel and a funny-shaped case long enough to have contained a gun. The passenger who claimed them was not anyone I'd ever seen. And he wasn't anyone I'd care to see again. He was tall, and he wore a black suit and one of those stovepipe hats. He looked like Abraham Lincoln, except that he had a mean-looking scowl on his face. I wondered what he was doing here—he didn't look like a man from the country. He didn't look like a man from the city either —not that I'd seen that many city men.

The train pulled out, and while the tall man in the black suit was talking to Mr. Guthrie, the depot agent, I started home. Instead of taking the main road, I decided to follow the railroad partway. Nearer home the track would cross the road at what we call Chinaberry Hollow because of the chinaberry trees that grow there. I would walk the rails that far. My brothers and I often did.

urging me to catch up—to follow the tracks, to see the country, to see the world. "At least see a mountain!" I said aloud.

I looked around sheepishly, as if sparrows in the weeds nearby might think me crazy for talking out loud, and I was so startled that I lost my balance and fell off the rail. I'd been so busy thinking about the outside world that I'd arrived at the main road without realizing it. A chinaberry tree was off to the side, but it was not the tree that startled me. It had been there for as long as I could remember. Standing beneath it, only a few feet away and looking straight at me, was the tall man in the black suit.

Sometimes we made a game of seeing who could walk a rail the furtherest and the fastest. I wasn't trying to set any record today, so I took my time. It was nice to hear the ringing in the rails from the train that had gone on down the tracks. Even my feet picked up a vibration from it.

I thought about the way the rails continued for miles and miles. I figured that if I had the strength I could walk anywhere in the country on them. Even if I had to keep one foot on the track at all times I could go from here to California. Or to Maine or Texas or any of those faraway places. Probably nobody could really do that. Still, it was fun to think about having superstrength and being able to go everywhere the tracks went. Sometimes I got the urge to keep walking—to see what was up ahead. Once I'd mentioned to my brothers that I wished I could follow the rails and always see what was over the next hill. Tyler said, "Matt Lindsey's place is over the next hill."

"Yeah," Skee said, "don't you remember? His chicken house is out nearly to the railroad track." Then Tyler said, "And if you'd like to know what's over the next hill after that, it's Elbert Mobley's place. His house is on one side of the track and his outhouse is on the other." When the railroad came, it had cut through the Mobleys' backyard and separated the home from the outbuilding, and Mr. Mobley had refused to relocate the outhouse. He insisted that it had been there first, and he and his family would just cross the railroad whenever they needed to make a trip to it.

"Oh, I didn't mean what was actually over the hill," I complained to my brothers.

"It's what you said you wished you could see," Tyler.

"I mean I wish I could go on and on and see lo places."

Tyler said, "Well, I don't care how many places saw, I doubt you'd find another one with the privy acr the track from a man's house." He and Skee had laugh and I hadn't said anything else to them about wanting follow the rails. But I had not stopped wanting to more than our red-clay hills.

The hills would get higher beyond Atlanta, I'd hear and gradually become mountains. I'd never seen a mou tain, but someday I would. I would see an ocean too, ar deserts, and jungles, and flatlands, and the Great Lake and all sorts of things I'd read about. There were time when I didn't know if I could wait much longer. I don' know what made me restless, even irritable sometimes My brothers and I got into fights more often than we used to. Mamma would say, "I don't know what's come over 'em," and Pa would laugh and say, "They're just acting like brothers, that's all." But that wasn't all. He was nearer right when he said, "They're growing up; they're changing, Ma. They're not little boys any more." Then he'd threaten to turn us across his knee and spank us as if we were.

As I walked along one of the rails I listened for the ringing sound. It was faint by now, but it was there all right. I could feel it even more than I could hear it. It was

: 89 :

Sometimes we made a game of seeing who could walk a rail the furtherest and the fastest. I wasn't trying to set any record today, so I took my time. It was nice to hear the ringing in the rails from the train that had gone on down the tracks. Even my feet picked up a vibration from it.

I thought about the way the rails continued for miles and miles. I figured that if I had the strength I could walk anywhere in the country on them. Even if I had to keep one foot on the track at all times I could go from here to California. Or to Maine or Texas or any of those faraway places. Probably nobody could really do that. Still, it was fun to think about having superstrength and being able to go everywhere the tracks went. Sometimes I got the urge to keep walking—to see what was up ahead. Once I'd mentioned to my brothers that I wished I could follow the rails and always see what was over the next hill. Tyler said, "Matt Lindsey's place is over the next hill."

"Yeah," Skee said, "don't you remember? His chicken house is out nearly to the railroad track." Then Tyler said, "And if you'd like to know what's over the next hill after that, it's Elbert Mobley's place. His house is on one side of the track and his outhouse is on the other." When the railroad came, it had cut through the Mobleys' backyard and separated the home from the outbuilding, and Mr. Mobley had refused to relocate the outhouse. He insisted that it had been there first, and he and his family would just cross the railroad whenever they needed to make a trip to it.

"Oh, I didn't mean what was actually over the next hill," I complained to my brothers.

"It's what you said you wished you could see," said Tyler.

"I mean I wish I could go on and on and see lots of places."

Tyler said, "Well, I don't care how many places you saw, I doubt you'd find another one with the privy across the track from a man's house." He and Skee had laughed, and I hadn't said anything else to them about wanting to follow the rails. But I had not stopped wanting to see more than our red-clay hills.

The hills would get higher beyond Atlanta, I'd heard, and gradually become mountains. I'd never seen a mountain, but someday I would. I would see an ocean too, and deserts, and jungles, and flatlands, and the Great Lakes, and all sorts of things I'd read about. There were times when I didn't know if I could wait much longer. I don't know what made me restless, even irritable sometimes. My brothers and I got into fights more often than we used to. Mamma would say, "I don't know what's come over 'em," and Pa would laugh and say, "They're just acting like brothers, that's all." But that wasn't all. He was nearer right when he said, "They're growing up; they're changing, Ma. They're not little boys any more." Then he'd threaten to turn us across his knee and spank us as if we were.

As I walked along one of the rails I listened for the ringing sound. It was faint by now, but it was there all right. I could feel it even more than I could hear it. It was urging me to catch up—to follow the tracks, to see the country, to see the world. "At least see a mountain!" I said aloud.

I looked around sheepishly, as if sparrows in the weeds nearby might think me crazy for talking out loud, and I was so startled that I lost my balance and fell off the rail. I'd been so busy thinking about the outside world that I'd arrived at the main road without realizing it. A chinaberry tree was off to the side, but it was not the tree that startled me. It had been there for as long as I could remember. Standing beneath it, only a few feet away and looking straight at me, was the tall man in the black suit.

12

Sailor with a Fiddle

"Scared you, didn't I?" said the man.

"Not much." I wondered if I should start running.

"Didn't mean to," he said, wiping perspiration from his forehead with a white handkerchief. "Stopped to cool a minute and to think a spell. Anybody home at the Todds'?"

I didn't answer. It didn't seem wise to tell a stranger, especially a scary-looking one, anything about our neighbors.

He asked louder, "Anybody home at the Todds'?"

"Somebody's home," I said. I reckoned I could find

help in the event he was out to do any harm to Miss Julia or Miss Etta.

"What's your name?" he asked.

"Wilkin Coley."

"God-hoss!" he said, smiling. "Grew up with your ma and pa." He didn't look nearly so scary when he smiled.

"Who are you?" I asked.

"Edgar Rounds. Better known as Cousin Edgar. Distantly related to everybody hereabouts. Close kin to none."

"I've heard of you," I said. "Didn't you go to sea when you were young?"

"Been at sea ever since," he said. "Got me a wife and two sons about your size in Brooklyn. Every now and then I check in with them; then I go back to sea." He looked around at the cropland off to one side of us and the pasture beyond. "On my way home now."

"To Brooklyn?" I asked. "It's a long way from here."

He laughed. "For years I've wanted to see these soft Georgia hills again, so I got off the ship in Savannah. I'll catch back up with it in Charleston and go on to New York."

"You've been to lots of places, I guess."

"All over the world."

"Some day I'll travel to far-off places," I said. "Maybe I'll go to sea."

"Wouldn't if I was you. You see too much sea and not enough world. Do it some other way."

"Well, I'm gonna get away from here," I said.

"Felt the same way when I was your age. Should have been content. Guess some of us are never satisfied." He looked now toward the woods on the other side of us. "Think before you leave all this. There's places more exciting, but none nicer." When he turned back to me, I noticed his gold tiepin. Ol' Tom Berle has a tiepin made from a one-dollar gold piece that he wears to church, but this one was much bigger.

"Is that a real gold piece?" I asked.

"Twenty-dollar one!" He took the pin from his tie and unclamped the small band that held the gold piece in place. "Have a look." He flipped the coin to me as if it were a penny. If I had missed the catch, it would have gone into high grass back of me. Cousin Edgar didn't seem concerned. "Minted in 1852."

I studied the coin on both sides and carefully handed it back to him. I wasn't about to toss it in the air. When he took it, he said, "Worth a lot more than twenty dollars now. Only thing I've ever held on to for long." He snapped it into the pin, which he put back on his tie. Then he picked up the satchel and the strange-looking case. When I glanced at the case, he explained, "Wouldn't go no place without my fiddle." He started walking, and I fell in beside him. I offered to carry the satchel or the fiddle case, but he said it balanced him to carry both.

"Old Man Todd died, didn't he?" he asked.

"A long time ago. Just his daughters there now."

"I'm hoping they'll put me up," he said. "They're about as close kin as I've got."

I didn't doubt but what they'd put him up, them being so hospitable and good. Still, I was surprised at the welcome he received when we got there. "Lord Mercy!" cried Miss Julia. "It's Cousin Edgar!" and she flung her arms around him and laughed and cried at the same time. Miss Etta came running out and did the same thing. I stood off to the side and watched. All three of them talked at once.

When I was about to start for home, Miss Etta said, "Be sure and tell your folks that Cousin Edgar's here."

"I'll tell 'em," I promised.

"Tell 'em we'll have a grand party while he's around. The whole community'll turn out!"

"Have to be tomorrow night," said Cousin Edgar. "Too late to get word around for tonight, and I can only stay two days."

The ladies started arguing with him. Surely he'd stay more than two days, they told him; he'd been gone such a long time. When he insisted that he couldn't stay longer, Miss Etta turned to me. "Party's tomorrow night. Help spread the word! Everybody's invited!"

"Even the Floyds?" I asked, certain that "everybody" meant "everybody but the Floyds," the way it usually did whenever there were community gatherings.

"Yes," said Miss Julia. "Let's include the Floyds. Lettie is Cousin Edgar's cousin too."

"How's she getting along?" he asked. "Is she still a beauty?"

Both women were silent, each one waiting for the other to answer. Finally Miss Etta said, "Lettie's had a

: 96 :

hard life. Ol' Damon and the oldest two boys are such scoundrels that they keep the family in disgrace. Lettie's been so embarrassed by their doings that she never gets out."

"That's a shame," said Cousin Edgar.

"And too, she's had a heart condition," said Miss Etta. "But maybe she'll come to a party in your honor. Wilkin, we appoint you to get word to her."

I didn't like the idea of going up to the Floyds' house and knocking on the door. Rip or Roger might think it'd be a good idea to beat me up. Me being littler than they are wouldn't make any difference to them; they're not noted for sportsmanship. Young didn't worry me too much. I could hold my own against him—maybe. Besides, he probably wasn't there. He wandered around more than he stayed home. I hoped his brothers were away too. It was so warm that I figured if they were home they'd be lying around on the porch or sitting in the shade of the big oak out front. Still, they might be inside, so I decided to yell from the yard. If they jumped me, I stood a chance of getting away.

"Anybody home?" I called. There was no answer. I called louder, "ANYBODY HOME?"

I heard a noise, like a chair falling backwards. Then there was silence. I called a third time, and the door opened. Mrs. Floyd stood just inside. Her hair was not combed, and she had on a flour-sack dress that was too big for her. It was hard to imagine that she had ever been a beauty. She said, "Yes?"

"Good afternoon," I said. "Miss Julia and Miss Etta Todd sent me up here with a message."

She stepped onto the porch. "I hope nothing's gone wrong." She had a soft voice.

"No, ma'am, something's gone right! They're having a party, and everybody's invited. It's tomorrow night, and they 'specially wanted me to get word to you."

"Thank you, honey, but tell 'em I don't get out." She smiled at me. "Can't remember when I've been to a party."

"This one's in honor of Cousin Edgar. He's come back from the sea." That sounded silly—as if he'd been under the ocean all these years. But Mrs. Floyd understood.

"Cousin Edgar," she said. "Is that a fact?" She looked out over the fields, then back at me. "We were young together." It was not only hard for me to imagine that Mrs. Floyd had ever been pretty; it was hard to imagine that she had ever been young. I didn't dwell on the thought, though, because I saw Rip and Roger coming down the road. If I could get out of the yard and head home, I might escape without them seeing me. So I said good day to Mrs. Floyd and started out. She called, "Thank you, honey, for coming by. Maybe some of us'll get to the party after all."

13

Up the Hanging Tree

"Quite a turnout!" said Pa. We were almost to the Todd house and could see that people were spilling over onto the big front porch.

"You'll be glad you came!" said Mamma. Pa had been so tired that he almost hadn't come with us.

Just then the music started, and he said, "I'm glad already. There's nothing like a hoedown to renew my strength!"

Mamma laughed. "Then let's join the dancers!" She handed me a tray of oatmeal-raisin cookies. "You boys take our things around back and into the dining room." She was talking about the cookies and a gallon of lemonade that Tyler was carrying. At gatherings like this everybody helps out with refreshments.

In the dining room the long table was filled with good things. Skee's eyes almost bugged out of his head. "My goodness!" he said. "When do we start on all this?"

Miss Julia, who was rearranging dishes to make room for a chocolate cake that Mrs. Spangler had just brought in, laughed. "Not yet awhile," she told Skee. "But won't it be grand when we do!"

Skee and Tyler went out through the kitchen. We'd seen Alex in the front yard, and they were going back to join him. I wanted to see the square dancing before I went outside, so I went up the hall to the big living room. Furniture had been pushed to the walls and the rugs taken away to leave a smooth floor with lots of room.

Cousin Edgar played his fiddle and Mrs. Ollie Jordon played the piano. Mrs. Asa Rogers strummed a banjo, and her husband did the calling. I looked around. It was fun to see grown-ups, who usually seemed so serious, shuffling about the dance floor having themselves a good time.

"Now dance with your corner lady!" called Mr. Rogers, and all the dancers changed partners.

It was then that I saw Mrs. Floyd. I almost didn't recognize her. Although her dress was a bit faded, she looked like anything but the drab woman I'd seen the afternoon before. Her hair was swept back and up into an interesting bun. A curly strand of it had come loose from the rest and bobbed up and down as she nodded to the other dancers and to friends on the sidelines. She was

:100:

greeted with comments like, "Good to see you, Lettie!" and "It's been a long time!" She smiled at each one, never missing a step, and suddenly I could imagine that once she really had been beautiful. Light from kerosene lamps did not show the worried lines in her face that I had seen in daylight. Or maybe they went away when she felt good. Somehow she looked happier than anyone I had ever seen. It could have been that she was happy because Ol' Damon and Rip and Roger hadn't done anything in a while to embarrass her. She could tell that her neighbors were glad to see her, and it was clear that she was glad to see them. Maybe she couldn't remember the last time she'd been to a party, but she was certainly enjoying this one.

Mrs. Floyd's partner was Mr. Ollie Jordon, whose wife was playing the piano, and when the dance ended they went over to chat with the musicians. As I went out to the porch I heard everyone telling Cousin Edgar how much like old times it was to have him around.

There was a crowd on the porch too. I saw Young Floyd out in the yard but was relieved when I didn't see Ol' Damon and Rip and Roger anywhere. On the rare occasions when they've been invited to parties, they've usually broken them up. Sometimes they broke them up when they weren't invited.

Edith Hurd, Polly Dade, and Fran Spangler were sitting in the big swing at the end of the porch. I waved at them, but they didn't let on that they saw me. Edith and I have been partial to one another at times, but she takes spells of being mad at me. Evidently this was one of

them, so I went into the yard, where Tyler and Skee, along with Young and Alex, were trying to decide what they wanted to do.

Young thought it would be a fine idea to sneak around back of the swing on the porch and turn it over. "Wilkin, you and Skee go pretend to be friendly with the girls, and I'll slip around to the other side if Tyler and Alex will help me, and we'll dump 'em out!"

"Let's do!" said Skee.

"And the girls would yell and scream," said Tyler. "Fran Spangler would probably pretend to be hurt so bad that she was dying, and the grown-ups would kick our butts and send us home."

"Well, I sure don't want to go home till I've had my fill of refreshments!" said Skee.

Young said, "Then let's slip into the house and load up on food. Then we'll turn over the swing!"

Alex said, "Everything you think about, Young, would bring on trouble!" While he was saying it he started walking away, and the rest of us followed him. I had no idea where he was going; I doubt that he did. But soon we were under the hanging tree. Alex propped himself against it, and the rest of us stood around him.

"Why don't somebody tell a ghost story?" said Young. "Maybe that'd make the ghost come out!"

"No self-respecting ghost would come out on a night like this," said Alex.

"Why not?" asked Young.

"For the same reason that even talk about ghosts ain't

scary; it's too bright. If it wasn't for the moonlight we might lure the ghost out."

Another of his ideas had been squelched, but Young did not give up. He suggested one crazy thing after another till finally he said, "I'll bet cain't nobody climb to the top of this tree."

"I'll bet I ain't gonna try," said Tyler.

"Me neither," echoed Skee.

"I doubt anybody could climb up to where the last big limbs fork out," said Alex.

That was all the challenge I needed. My brothers admitted that they didn't have the nerve to try it, and Alex doubted that it could be done. Instead of saying anything, I sprang to the lowest branch, swung onto it, and was climbing through the limbs before anyone realized what I was doing. I made my way slowly, one branch after another. In the daytime it might have worried me to see the ground at such a distance, but everything looked soft in the moonlight.

"You'd better turn around," called Tyler. "It's foolish to climb any higher." But I kept going. I could hear Skee saying, "When Wilkin makes up his mind to do something, ain't nothing can change it."

Near the top of the tree, just as I caught hold of a limb overhead, the branch on which I was standing gave way. It went crashing to the ground. Even in moonlight that was scary. I held fast to the limb above me and tried to pull myself up.

"Hey!" yelled Tyler. "Quit kicking dead limbs down here!"

:105:

"We'll throw the next one back at you!" shouted Young. "Part of it almost hit me!"

Eventually I struggled onto the next branch, my strength almost gone. I drew a couple of deep breaths and then made my way to the fork at the top. "Well, I'm here!" I called.

Skee sighed as if he couldn't believe I had climbed so high, and Tyler yelled, "You made it!"

Alex said, "That's *some* climbing!"

The only one not impressed was Young. He said, "I could do it if I tried."

Alex said, "But you didn't try, and Wilkin did." I was proud to hear him taking up for me.

Just then Miss Julia called from the front porch: "Boys! Where are you?"

"We're here," yelled Alex.

"Refreshment time!" shouted Miss Julia. "Hurry! Hurry!"

"C'mon, let's go!" said Young.

Tyler called to me, "We're going back to the house!"

"Hey, wait!" I yelled. "I'm coming down."

"We'll wait at the house," said Skee. "At the refreshment table!"

The moon was going behind a cloud, and I yelled, "It's getting dark."

Young called back, "We had a cat that stayed up in a tree three days once."

"If you're not down in three days, we'll come looking for you," said Tyler. All of them laughed as they hurried to the house.

:106:

The moon completely disappeared, and I couldn't see. Resting in the top of the tree I waited . . . and waited, but there was no sign of the moon. Finally I started feeling my way down. I hung from a limb and dangled my feet until they found a solid place on the branch below. Then I eased down to it, and felt for a lower branch. Three times the system worked, then suddenly I dangled in the air with no footing to be found. This would be where the limb had broken; naturally there was a gap! I pulled myself back onto the branch above me and crawled toward the trunk. I could huddle there till the moon came out. Without light I couldn't see a lower branch well enough to risk jumping onto it.

Although it was a warm night, I shivered. The thought of the ghost didn't worry me. As Alex had said, a ghost wouldn't come out on a night like this. *Wait a minute!* I thought. The ghost wouldn't come out because of moonlight, but there was no moonlight now.

Then I noticed a flicker of light in the distance. The night was dark again, then another flicker, this time followed by a rumbling noise. It was lightning and thunder.

There was another flicker way off on the horizon—and another. I clung to the branch, knowing that if a storm was gathering, the moon would not appear. But a ghost might!

14

The Theft

The lightning ended and the night was darker than ever —dark and silent. Then I heard a thin, rattling noise. It was nearby, and I was scared enough to jump—but sensible enough to know better. So I huddled against the trunk of the tree. Everything was quiet again; then, *rattle . . . rattle.*

The sound came at intervals, and I felt chilled. The breeze had picked up each time I heard it, so it was the breeze that put a chill on me—not fright, although I admit to being scared.

It seemed as if the rattle prompted the wind to blow, but I realized it was the other way around. The next time

I heard the sound I reached out in the direction of it. My hand came onto a cluster of dry leaves. I crushed them in my fist, and the sound ended. The night was so quiet then that I would have welcomed the rustling leaves back. I thought of the ghost and felt chilled, even though the wind had died down. I even thought I heard footsteps, but ghosts floated.

A beam of light flashed through the tree, and someone said, "Are you up there, Cowboy?" Of course it was Alex.

"I'm here."

"I borrowed Mr. Dade's big flashlight," he said. Mr. Dade doctors horses and cows, and he has a box-type flashlight to use whenever he makes night calls.

"I can climb down if you'll keep the light on the limb just below me," I yelled. "There, hold it right there!"

"Are you sure it's not too far?"

I was already hanging from the branch on which I'd been sitting, ready to drop to the next one. "I'll land on it," I said. "I've got to!" At that, I let go. One foot landed all right; the other one slipped. I slid from the branch but managed to grab it with my hands, scratching both arms. I hung on.

The next branch was nearer. By stretching I was able to set my feet firmly on it before letting go of the one above.

"Easy now . . . easy . . . easy!" cautioned Alex.

Finally I made it, sprawling onto the ground when I dropped from the lowest limb. Alex laughed. "You climb to the top and back like a monkey, but you can't stand on solid ground!" He helped me to my feet and brushed off my back.

"When you didn't show up inside," he explained, "I figured you might not be able to get down without some light."

We started toward the house. Halfway there we met Tyler and Skee. They had our flashlight and were coming to check on me.

Tyler said, "We figured we'd let you get scared a little. Then maybe you'd learn a lesson about being too stubborn to ever change your mind once you set out to do something." That could have been the start of a fight, but I was too glad to be on the ground to get mad. "C'mon," he said. "Let's go back inside."

I was pleased that Alex and my brothers had come back to see what had happened to me. Only Young Floyd had not concerned himself. He was on the front porch eating pound cake when we got there. Greedy as always, he had a handful of cookies too.

Miss Etta came to the doorway. "Come in, Wilkin," she said. "You must have some refreshments! I believe the other boys have already found their way to the table."

"Yes, ma'am," said Skee, "but we wouldn't mind finding our way to it again."

Miss Etta laughed. "There's certainly plenty! Why don't all of you go back?"

Alex said he'd had all he wanted, and Young, of course, had all that he could manage at the moment. Tyler and Skee went with me to the dining room, where we ate caramel cake, our favorite, and drank lemonade.

There was a lot of milling around, and while Tyler, Skee, and I were standing near the table, Cousin Edgar and Pa came over to us. "These are my three," said Pa.

"Met the middle one yesterday," said Cousin Edgar, nodding at me. "Glad to see all of you!" After he had shaken our hands, he and Pa started talking to each other again.

Skee interrupted them: "Cousin Edgar, Wilkin told us about that big ol' gold piece you've got. You wouldn't happen to be wearing it, would you?"

Cousin Edgar laughed. "Started out the night with a coat and tie, but got too warm about the third set. Took 'em off and put 'em up."

"Well, I'm sorry I missed out on seeing that fine stickpin," said Skee.

"You haven't missed out," said Cousin Edgar. "Come along, we'll have a look at it now."

He took one of the lamps from the dining room table and led the way up the hall. Just as we started into the guest room, Young Floyd came out of it.

"What are you doing in here?" asked Cousin Edgar.

"Nothin'," said Young. "I was just going back to the porch."

"The porch is out there!" said Cousin Edgar a bit crossly.

Young left, and Cousin Edgar went over to the small table beside the bed. "Here's my tie," he said. "The pin'll be here somewhere." After a moment he added, "But it's not." He looked for it on the floor. Then he checked the bedside table again and had Tyler and me look under the bed to see if anything had fallen beneath it.

"You're sure you brought it in here?" asked Pa.

"Positive!" said Cousin Edgar. "You don't suppose that boy took it, do you?"

"Young Floyd'd do anything," said Skee.

Pa scolded him. "Now, Skee!"

"Surely he wouldn't steal," said Cousin Edgar, just as Alex came into the room.

When nobody else commented, Alex said, "It didn't just walk off."

"No, it didn't," agreed Cousin Edgar.

"We'll have to ask the boy," said Pa, as if he really hated to do it.

"Nothing else to do," agreed Cousin Edgar.

They called Young to come into the room. If he had come immediately, there might not have been as much commotion. But Young called back, "I don't want to."

Pa said firmly, "Come anyway!" and I heard Mrs. Floyd in the living room say, "Go on, Young, honey, they're a-wanting you."

"I ain't done nothin'," protested Young, stumbling into the room a moment later, urged forward by Mr. Dade and Mr. Jordon, one on each side of him.

When Cousin Edgar and Pa asked Young about the gold piece he denied ever having seen it. "You can search me," he said.

Of course, by then he'd had time to take anything outside and hide it till later. He said he'd only been in the room because Alex had put him up to going into it.

:112:

"But I didn't take nothin'," he insisted.

Pa asked, "Are you sure?" and Young screamed, "I ain't done nothin'! You cain't put nothin' on me!" so loud that everybody began gathering in the bedroom to see what was the matter. The room became so crowded that I stood in the hallway.

Mrs. Floyd looked crushed when she realized what was going on. I guess she'd had practice in being disappointed in her menfolks, but somehow it didn't seem right that Young should be embarrassing her now.

Young continued to deny that he knew anything about the gold piece. After a while his mother said, "If he says he didn't take it, then he didn't take it." Her voice trembled slightly, but she regained control of it as she added, "And it's time for us to be going. I'm sorry we came."

Miss Julia reached out and patted her. "We're glad you came, Lettie. It's been so long."

Mrs. Floyd said, "Come on, Young!" and she led him from the room. She held her head high, but as she came into the hallway I saw tears starting to roll down her cheeks. No one in the room could have seen them, and I wished that I couldn't have.

15

Anything but Pulling Fodder

Alex and I walked to Blyden's Crossing with Cousin Edgar the next morning and waited with him on the platform. "I'm one gold piece lighter than I was yesterday," he said, "but *things* are not what matter most. People and places are what really count." Looking out across the fields and pastures, he said, "These beautiful red-clay hills!" I wondered why, if he loved Georgia so much, he'd ever left—or why he didn't come back to stay. As if he knew what had gone through my mind, he said, "Of course, there are lots of interesting places." Then he got back to the gold piece. "If Lettie's boy stole it, it'll do him more harm than good."

I expected him to say that in some foreign port a curse had been put on the gold piece that would bring disaster to anyone except its rightful owner. Maybe it had already got back at Young Floyd in some way. I hoped so. Alex said, "You mean it's got a hex on it?" He sounded alarmed.

Cousin Edgar laughed. "No, nothing like that! I only meant that anybody who steals something is worse off eventually than if he hadn't. We all have to walk in our own integrity."

Alex and I looked puzzled, and Cousin Edgar explained: "Picked that phrasing up from the Bible. It means that each one of us has to live with ourself. If we cheat or lie or steal, then we know that what we're living with is low-down, whether anybody else does or not. And if you don't respect yourself, life is miserable." He added just as the train whistle sounded, "Still, I'm sorry that it was Lettie's boy." He gazed into the distance a moment without saying anything. I figured he was about to comment on Georgia countryside again, but he said softly, "Lettie and I were young together." He sounded like Mrs. Floyd when she'd said the same thing—as if they hadn't been young with anyone else.

The train arrived, and he boarded it. In Atlanta he'd take another train to Charleston, and in Charleston he'd catch his ship to Brooklyn. I wished I could go to Charleston and catch a ship. Instead I went home and started pulling fodder.

Pulling fodder is as dreary a job as there is. We pulled the leaves from the cornstalks and formed them into small bundles by tying one leaf around the others. After they were tied, we hooked them back onto the stalk and left them there to dry. Later the small bundles would be bunched together into bigger ones and stored in barn lofts and feedrooms. Fodder's used like hay in feeding mules and cows. The ears of corn are harvested in the fall, but fodder-pulling is done in late summer.

Finally we caught up on our crop and hired out to Mr. Madden to help with his. It was not as interesting as helping him in early summer—not nearly as sociable. Big Will was busy with his own corn crop, so we missed him and Edna and Katie. Alex, when he wasn't working at the store, was helping Miss Julia plant a late garden and do some painting around the house. Not even Mr. Madden was with us; he was breaking up new ground for fall wheat. Only my brothers and I were in the field, and we were tired of the work and each other. The pace was slow, and the weather was hot. August never has been my favorite month anyway. I always begin to get restless, anxious to start on something new—even school. "At least when school starts we'll see a few more people," I said, talking to Alex one night when I was spending the night with him.

"In Atlanta you could see even more people," he said. "Let's you and me go to the city."

"Maybe Ma and Pa'd let me," I said, "since I'd be with you and you know your way around. They always say, 'You'd get lost,' whenever I ask about spending a day up there."

: *117* :

"I'm not talking about a day," said Alex. "Let's run away and live in Atlanta."

I was sure he was kidding, but I went along with the joke. "You could go back to your mother's house," I said, "but where would I live?"

"I ain't going back home," he said. "Me and you both could stay at the hotel."

"Yeah, I know," I said, laughing. "What are we gonna do, rob a bank or something?"

"Not right away," he said, laughing too. "But we really could live at the hotel—the one where I worked before. They've got a big room in the basement with bunks in it where the help can sleep during off-duty hours. The night manager let me sleep there lots of times. If we worked for him, he'd find a place for us."

"But comes next month we'll have to go to school."

"Well, they've got schools in Atlanta. Good ones, I guess, as far as schools go, but we wouldn't have to go. We can get jobs as bellhops from the middle of the afternoon till midnight; that's the busiest time anyway. Anybody'll naturally think we're in school the rest of the day. What they don't know is none of their business!"

"I'd want to go to school," I said. "At least I guess I would." I never had thought of *not* going. I thought of it now, and the idea was interesting.

"Well, you can go," said Alex. "The night manager might have to sign as your guardian; he signed for one of the boys last year. It wasn't exactly legal, but he got by with it."

Alex sounded serious, and although I wasn't I acted as

:118:

if I were when he started telling about all the things we could do in our spare time. He said we could go to picture shows. I couldn't imagine being able to go to a picture show whenever the notion struck me. A tent movie comes to town every summer, and the few movies I've ever seen have been in it. Of course the same thing that has kept me from going often to tent movies might hold me back in the city—lack of the price of admission. But times are better now that I'm big enough to hire out for field work. I even have a little money saved up, and I'd earn more as a bellhop.

"We could go out and climb Stone Mountain," said Alex. "It's the eighth wonder of the world."

Of course I'd heard about Stone Mountain. Every year the seniors at County High have a field trip, and they go to Stone Mountain. I hated having to wait till I was a senior in high school to see it.

Just then we heard a knock at the back door. Alex got up and started putting on his clothes to answer it, but Miss Etta got there first. We heard her talking to someone, and after a while we heard Miss Julia too. It sounded as if Miss Julia was leaving with the caller. She has a talent as a nurse, and every now and then Dr. Sanders sends for her when he needs help. I figured somebody was having a baby.

We heard Miss Etta going back to the front part of the house, and Alex started talking about Atlanta again. "Grants Park is something else you'll like," he said. "The zoo is there."

"Really?"

Alex laughed. "That's right, you've never been to one, have you?" When I didn't say anything he added, "Why, you've never even seen a lion or a tiger!"

"I've seen a monkey," I said crossly. He didn't need to remind me of what I hadn't seen. "And I've seen a trained bear. A peddler came through here with one once and stopped at Larson's store. If I'd had a dime I could have seen it drink milk from a bottle just like a baby; that's what the man said it could do."

Maybe I sounded angry, because Alex said, "I ain't making fun of you, Cowboy. I'm just telling you what all's in a zoo." I knew what was in a zoo. I just never had *seen* what was in a zoo. But I'd seen pictures, and sometimes I did have an awful urge to see more than just pictures.

"And there's Candler Field," said Alex. "That's the airport, and we can catch a trolley to it some Sunday when we're not working and watch planes take off and land."

I didn't let on that I was too impressed, but I knew it would be a splendid sight to see a lot of airplanes. I've never seen but one. It landed by accident in Mr. Alan Dodson's pasture two years ago. When a small crowd gathered to see it, the pilot took passengers up for a ride if they had money to pay him. It had been as exciting a time around here as I can remember, even though I'd been flat broke and didn't get to go up in the plane. I told Alex, "Maybe if we saved up enough money, one Sunday when we're at Candler Field we can take us a ride."

"Sure, Cowboy," he said, and I realized that I was no

longer just pretending to be serious. I went to sleep thinking about all the things there are to do in the world. And too, I told myself that I might like working as a bellhop. Anything beat pulling fodder.

16

Plans

At daybreak I punched Alex. "Time to wake up!" He rolled over and groaned. I got up and dressed. "So long!" I called, not waiting for an answer. He wouldn't go back to sleep. It was time to do the morning's chores, and he knew there was no holding back the day.

Starting through the kitchen, I was surprised to see Miss Julia sitting at the table. A cup of coffee was in front of her. Although her eyes were open, she did not appear to see me.

"Miss Julia! Are you all right?"

She jumped. "Oh!"

"I didn't mean to scare you."

She reached out and pulled me to her. "It's all right," she said, but I knew that it wasn't. I put my arm around her shoulders and patted her. She was taking a sip of coffee when Alex came in.

"Is something wrong?" he asked.

Miss Julia put down her cup. "Lettie died," she said. Then she repeated it: "Lettie died. There was nothing Dr. Sanders could do to save her." She leaned forward, and her head slumped onto the table.

"She's fainted," said Alex. "I'll call Miss Etta."

Later, when Miss Julia had revived and Miss Etta was in the kitchen, we talked more. Miss Etta said, "Some will say Lettie overdid it by dancing so much the night of our party."

"It doesn't matter what *some say,*" said Miss Julia. "Lettie had a heart condition, but who knows whether she should have been more careful."

I said, "Young killed her! It wasn't dancing that hurt her at the party. It was Young."

"Now, now!" said Miss Julia. "Don't sit in judgment."

During the morning Mamma made potato salad and baked an apple pie. It's a custom to send such things to homes where there has been a death.

Tyler delivered the food in the afternoon, and that night Mamma and Pa put on their Sunday clothes and went to the Floyds' to pay their respects. The next day all of us went to the funeral.

We got home by midafternoon and Tyler, Skee, and I worked on the pasture fence for a while and then did our

: 123 :

regular chores. I made the mistake of finishing mine first. "Good!" said Mamma. "I was hoping one of you would have time to run up to the Floyds'."

"What for?"

"To tell Young to come stay with us anytime he'd like. I can't help worrying about him."

"You can't tell him that! He's liable to move in with us."

"Anybody else would have relatives to help them out," said Mamma, "but I doubt any of their kin will be so obliging. Ol' Damon and the older boys can make do for themselves, but Young's only a child."

"He's fourteen," I said. "Let him make do for himself too."

"His mother's gone," said Mamma. "Now do as I say!" So I went to the Floyds'.

It was late afternoon and almost dark when I got there. Ol' Damon was sitting on the front porch. "The boys are inside," he said. At least that's what I think he said. He half-mumbled, half-growled something.

Rip and Roger, in the kitchen, stood across a table from each other. Young sat in a corner. Just as I walked in, Roger yelled, "It ain't so!" He threw out his right fist, landing it upside Rip's jaw. Rip spun around, grabbed the back of a chair to steady himself, and then threw the chair at Roger. I hurried out!

Ol' Damon called, "Shut up in there!" as I went past him. I didn't slow down till I was on the road. When I realized that someone was close on my heels, I speeded up again.

: 124 :

Someone called, "Wait a minute, Wilkin!" and I realized it was Young. "What did you come over to the house for?" he asked, when I had stopped and turned around.

"Mamma sent me."

"How come?"

"She said to tell you to feel welcome to our house anytime you'd like to visit us."

"I'll go now," he said, starting ahead. "What's she cooking for supper?"

"Oh, she didn't necessarily mean right now," I said, catching up with him.

"It's a good time to go," said Young. "Maybe Rip and Roger'll kill each other. Them and Pa's been drinking whisky ever since we got home from the cemetery."

"Hadn't you better go back and tell your Pa where you've gone?"

"No, he don't care. Besides, he'll soon be too drunk to know whether I'm there or not."

There was no talking him out of going home with me, so I walked along beside Young as if we were friends. I felt sorry for him, losing his mother, but that didn't prompt me to forget how much I disliked him. One minute I could see Mrs. Floyd, dancing and smiling, and the next minute I saw her face streaked with tears. I hated Young for the pain he had caused her.

At home during supper my opinion of Young did not change. Mamma had fried a chicken, which is always a special treat, and Young helped himself to both drumsticks when the platter was passed to him first. I wound up with a wing and the gizzard.

Mamma and Pa invited Young to spend the night, but he declined. He said his father and brothers would be passed out by then, so he'd just go ahead home. Mamma told him to come back anytime he'd like.

Afterwards he came for supper often, and although Mamma finally got the idea across to him that he should leave a little food for everybody else, he was still obnoxious as far as I was concerned.

One afternoon just at suppertime Skee and I were in the backyard. I was cutting kindling, and he was stacking it for us to take inside. We have to keep a supply of it in the kitchen for starting fires in the cookstove. When I was almost finished, Young came along, carrying a bunch of cardinal flowers—the biggest, prettiest ones I'd ever seen. They grow in the swamp and are not common even there. I had seen a few in years past, but evidently Skee had not. "What are *those*?" he asked.

"They're flowers," said Young. I might have thought he was giving Skee a smart-alecky answer, but from the way he said it I realized that he didn't know what kind they were but prided himself in knowing they were something special. Just then Mamma opened the door.

"Why, Young!" she said, looking at the brilliant red blooms. "How beautiful!" I wished then that I had gone into the swamp to find her some of the flowers. It somehow didn't seem right that Young should have thought of it.

"I brung 'em to you," said Young, holding the bouquet out to her. "They was Mamma's favorites, and,

: 126 :

well. . . ." He slowed down, and I thought for a minute he was going to cry. I guess thinking about his mother was not easy. He cleared his throat and started over. "They was Mamma's favorites, and I thought you might like 'em too."

"I love them!" said Mamma, taking the flowers from him. "And I've never seen prettier ones. I'll put them in the middle of the table for us to enjoy while we're having supper. You'll eat with us, won't you?"

"I was aiming to," he said, following her into the house. He could have at least taken a load of kindling inside at the same time.

I began to spend a lot of my spare time at the Todds'. In the afternoons when I had finished the day's work I went up there. Miss Julia always asked me to stay for supper, and I accepted as often as my folks would let me.

Whenever Alex and I had a chance to be by ourselves we talked about running away. We agreed that we'd catch the freight train that came through Blyden's Crossing near midnight. I figured we were talking about a long time off, but it was fun to think about being in Atlanta. The thought was exciting and a bit scary at the same time.

I was careful not to tell Tyler or Skee about the plan. Tyler would try to talk me out of it. He'd say it didn't make sense, and we'd probably get in a fight. I'm not sure what Skee would have said. He might have wanted to go with us—or he might have told Mamma and Pa.

Late one afternoon Alex came out to the garden while Skee and I were hoeing the late crop of tomatoes. It was a job Pa had said we must complete that day *without fail*.

"You finished your chores already?" I asked.

"All but feeding the shoats," he said. "I just thought I'd step down here and see what all's going on."

"Nothing's going on," said Skee. "Didn't you know that? Nothing ever happens around here!"

Alex and I laughed, and I said, "For once, Skee's right!"

"Of course," said Skee, "there *was* the party when Cousin Edgar was here; that was a good one—till Young Floyd stole the gold piece." He propped himself on the hoe and added, "And other things come along from time to time. There's to be a 4-H Club rally before school starts. That's always fun. And the church may have a picnic. I guess I'll have to take it back about nothing ever happening."

"Why don't you go to the house and think up a few other events to add to your social calendar," I said.

"I can think of 'em right here," he said. I knew there was no way of running him off, but he surprised me. "On the other hand," he said, "I'm not one to hang around where I'm not welcome." That was a lie. He's always been one to hang around whether welcome or not, and I should have known he was up to something. He took his hoe and started toward the house. At the end of the garden he called, "Of course, this means you've gotta finish hoeing out the tomatoes by yourself."

"It does not!"

: 129 :

"It does so! You chased me off!" At that he started running.

"You come back!" I yelled, but Alex said, "Let him go. I need to talk to you."

He sounded as if he had something urgent on his mind, so I didn't run after Skee. Maybe something had gone wrong at the store. "The debt," as Mr. Larson had called it, was to have been paid up last week; that had been the bargain. Alex had worked two months for nothing. From then on, he was to have been paid. Maybe Mr. Larson was being slow to remember the terms of the agreement. I hoped they were not having trouble, but I knew that I'd have trouble if I didn't finish the tomatoes.

I hated to be tricked into doing more than my share of the work, but Skee would win any argument about it if I didn't. He would say that Alex and I wanted to get rid of him, and he'd be right. And I'd be punished. "I'll have to keep working," I said, "or Pa'll blister my seat."

"Never mind," said Alex. "You won't be here to worry about it."

"How come?"

"That's what I came to tell you. Tonight's the night we run away!"

"Not tonight; I'm not ready. Besides, we gotta make plans."

"We've made 'em: we catch the midnight freight." He turned to leave.

"Hey, wait a minute!"

"I gotta get back," he said, "or Miss Etta and Miss Julia'll wonder what's become of me. After supper I'll tell 'em that I'm gonna spend the night with you. And you tell your folks that you're gonna spend the night with me. That way, nobody'll be suspicious. I'll wait for you under the hanging tree."

"We've got to shell butterbeans after supper so Mamma'll be able to can 'em tomorrow. What if I can't get away?"

"I'll go without you," he said. "And you can bury yourself in this place forever. Dig your own grave, Cowboy!"

17

Pistol Shot

One minute I'd think about how much fun it would be to live in Atlanta; the next minute I'd wonder if maybe I shouldn't stay home. Then I'd think about Atlanta again and all the exciting things I'd heard about it. Of course, city life might not be as wonderful as I'd pictured it, but one thing was certain: I wouldn't know what it was like if I stayed home forever.

During supper I was thinking about going away, persuading myself that it was the thing to do, instead of listening to a family discussion. I didn't even know what Pa was talking about when he asked, "Don't you think so, Wilkin?" Fortunately, Skee interrupted to ask a question, and no one knew I hadn't been paying attention.

After we'd eaten, Skee began clearing the table, and Tyler got out the dishpan. It wasn't my turn to help with the dishes, so I went to the bedroom and gathered up a few clothes to take to Atlanta. I tried to bundle them together, but they kept falling apart no matter how I tied them. Finally I slipped out to the barn with them, and in the feedroom I found a burlap bag that would do as a knapsack.

After I'd stuffed the clothes into it, I took the bag to the backyard and was hiding it under the corner of the house when Mamma called, "Where are you, Wilkin?"

"I'm here," I said.

"C'mon!" she called. "The fun's beginning!" She was making a joke. It was time to start the night's work.

Soon it was dark, and Tyler lit the big lamp in the middle of the table. We sat around it, shelling the butterbeans. Even Pa joined in. I used to like it whenever he helped us. He'd tell stories about how things used to be. Sometimes we'd sing and play guessing games while we worked. But this time I wasn't interested in anything but getting the job done. Atlanta was waiting for me! I had never shelled butterbeans faster.

Skee took pains to shell the last pod so that he could hold it up and say, "This is the one we've been looking for!" as if he had made up the remark. Tyler and I hauled the shells to the backyard, and when we were back inside I said, "I forgot to say that I'm spending the night with Alex."

Mamma said, "You mean you forgot to ask permission!"

"You never have objected to any of us spending the night at the Todds'."

"No, but usually you go right after supper. It's too late now."

"Then I'd better go tell 'em I'm not coming. They'll be waiting up for me."

Pa said, "You should have told 'em you couldn't make it tonight. You knew your Ma had work laid out for us."

"I won't do it again," I promised.

"You'd better go ahead up there this time," said Pa, "or Etta and Julia'll wait up all night. Just get home in time to do your work in the morning."

"Yes, sir, I will," I said. I had never failed to get home in time to do the early-morning chores, and it irritated me that Pa should always remind me.

On the way through the kitchen I took my toothbrush from the top of the washstand. "Hey," called Skee, peering at me, "how come you're taking your toothbrush?"

"To brush my teeth with!" I said.

"But you've already brushed your teeth," he said. We always brush our teeth soon after supper to get it over with. "Don't you remember?"

"I remember," I said disgustedly, pretending to put back the toothbrush but palming it till I could get outside.

I thought Skee was fooled, but when I was at the corner of the house, reaching for my belongings, I heard him in the kitchen saying, "Look! He took his toothbrush anyway!" Now I was trapped. Mamma and Pa would know something was up, and in a moment they'd be looking for me. Skee persisted: "Reckon why he took his toothbrush?"

"To brush his teeth, dumbbell!" said Tyler. "He told you so!"

"Now, boys!" said Mamma. "Knowing Etta and Julia as I do, they'll probably have a snack of some sort for the boys at bedtime. It's just as well that Wilkin is concerned about caring for his teeth." Then she teased Skee: "I won't mention any names, but wouldn't it be nice if everybody were concerned about such things?" Skee always had to be reminded, and reminded again—and sometimes forced—to brush his teeth. Mamma's comment quieted him down for a moment. I was starting away when he said, "Maybe I just ought to go up there and spend the night too. I expect Miss Julia cooked up something good to serve them. I'll take my toothbrush along, okay?"

"No," said Mamma, "not tonight."

Pa said, "Maybe you ought to go up there, Skeedy, and ask the ladies if they've made any cookies lately. And bring us a plateful down here!"

"Pa!" said Mamma. "You know better than to put an idea like that in Skee's head!"

"He knows I'm teasing."

"He should. But sometimes you give him ideas." When I left, she was reminding Skee that Pa had not been serious.

:136:

There was a full moon, and I didn't have to use the flashlight at first. Then the moon went behind a cloud, and I turned the flashlight on. A moment later I remembered that Miss Etta and Miss Julia didn't know I was going to be out; they thought Alex was at our house. If they happened to see a light in the grove, they might wonder what was wrong. So I turned it off and made my way in darkness.

There was a silvery shape beneath the hanging tree, which would be Alex, wearing a white shirt. He had scared me a few times by jumping out at me; this would be my chance to get back at him. The moon reappeared, and I slipped into the edge of the woods and gradually made my way toward Alex. I picked up a small stone and tossed it at the trunk of the hanging tree. It would take Alex by surprise, but it took me by surprise too! Just as it struck the tree there was a loud noise as if the stone had exploded—or a shot had been fired.

"Don't move or I'll shoot again," a voice called. I recognized it as Miss Etta's. She was on the other side of the hanging tree, coming along the path from the house.

"It's just me," called Alex. "Don't shoot!"

Miss Etta laughed. "I figured who it'd be. But when I saw a light flashing down here I thought I'd better check. I like to try out the pistol every few months to make sure it's still working." By then she was under the tree. "You boys sort of sneaked off from home, huh?" She looked around. "Where are the others?"

Alex said, "It's just me. . . ."

I stepped underneath the hanging tree. "And me," I said.

"We were thinking of going frog-gigging one night," explained Alex, sounding relieved that I had shown up. "And we decided to go down to the creek and see how many frogs are around."

"Figured Julia'd say no, it was dangerous, huh?" said Miss Etta, laughing. "And Wilkin's folks might say the same thing? So both of you slipped off!" We saw a lantern bobbing along the path out toward the road, and Miss Etta called, "Who's that?"

"It's me," answered Pa, and Miss Etta hurried out the path to meet him. Alex and I stayed where we were, but we could hear them talking.

"I heard a shot," said Pa. "Anything wrong?"

"Nothing serious," said Miss Etta. "Something's been getting our chickens that roost in the trees these warm nights. I heard one of 'em squawking and thought I glimpsed a fox heading toward the woods. Figured a shot in the air might scare it away for a while." She thanked Pa for his concern, and he told her that he was glad there was no real trouble.

The moon disappeared just as Miss Etta returned to the hanging tree. "I didn't tell on you." she said. "And don't you tell Julia on me! If anything should go wrong she'd blame me for not stopping you. I'll go in now and tell her how I almost shot the fox!"

18

The Woods at Night

Miss Etta turned up the wick of her lantern and started back toward the house. Alex and I headed into the woods as if we really were on our way to the creek. Alex called to Miss Etta, "One night soon we'll have a frog-leg supper!"

"Sounds good!" she called back.

I could see the light from her lantern bobbing up and down as she made her way along the path. A moment later it stopped, although she was still some distance from the house. The light did not go out, but it was still. "Something's happened to Miss Etta," I said.

"How can you tell?"

"The light's quit moving. Reckon she fell down? She might've twisted an ankle; we'd better go see about her."

"She'll be okay," said Alex.

We watched a moment, and when the light still didn't move I said, "I'm going to see if she's all right." I started away, but Alex didn't follow me.

Before I had gone far, the lantern light began to bob along again, and I knew Miss Etta was fine. She must have just stopped to rest. I went back to where I'd left Alex, but he wasn't there.

"Alex?" I called. "Where are you?"

"Over here," he answered. He was nearby, I was certain, but I couldn't see him. "Wait there," he said, "I'm coming over."

I shone my light through the trees but couldn't spot him. Vines hanging down from overhead and patches of tall briers made it difficult to see.

"Be careful!" I warned. "That old well is in here somewhere. We're close to it."

Just then I heard a loud splash and a hollow echo like something heavy hitting the water in the bottom of the well.

"Alex?" I called. "Alex? Are you okay?"

There was no answer.

Quickly I found the well and called again. Still there was no answer. Frantic, I lay on the ground at the rim of the well and shone my flashlight inside it. All I could see were the walls. They looked as if they were about to cave in. I pushed myself away from the edges when a

clod of loose earth fell into the well. "Alex?" I yelled shrilly. "Are you down there?"

He answered calmly from back of me, "No, I'm here." He stepped out from behind a tree.

I got up and brushed myself off. Neither of us said anything till I asked angrily, "What was it?"

"What was what?"

"What was it that hit the water?"

"A rotten log. I kicked it in." When I didn't say anything, he added, "I almost stumbled over it. I kicked it accidentally."

"Yeah, I guess you hid accidentally too! And you didn't answer when I called *accidentally*. You thought it was a good joke."

"Wasn't it?" he asked, adding before I could answer, "C'mon, let's get back to the hanging tree and pick up our stuff."

I stalked past him, but by the time we were at the edge of the woods I was in a better humor. The moon had come out, and a mockingbird in a holly tree sang a lively night song.

"You're too noisy," said Alex, chunking a stone at the base of the holly tree.

"Don't do that!" I said to Alex. Then I called, "Sing on, bird!" The bird burst out singing. Alex and I both laughed.

After we had gathered up our belongings I started back toward the Todds'.

"Hey," said Alex, "you're going the wrong way." I stopped and looked at him. "C'mon," he said, slinging his

:142:

knapsack across his shoulder, "let's get going. If we fool around we'll miss the train."

"You mean you're still planning to go tonight?"

"*We're* still planning to go," he said, starting toward the road.

I hurried to catch up. "But the night's half gone."

"No, it's just that a lot has happened in a little while. There's still time."

Along the way I argued that we should wait till another time: Any venture that got off to a troublesome start was bound to be unlucky. Alex wanted to know when I had become superstitious. Anyway, it was just that all our bad luck had come first, he insisted; it would be good times from now on.

Ahead of us, a car came over a hill. We saw the lights and jumped off the road. Alex lay in the ditch, and I hid behind a thicket of sumacs. Being sneaky was not to my liking, but for the time being it was necessary.

While waiting for the car to go past, I thought of my folks. I wondered if they'd understand why I had run away. Would they somehow know that it was because of an urge—a real, deep-down longing—to start seeing more of the world than just our bit of it? Or would they think I hated home? I hoped they'd understand, but maybe they wouldn't. It worried me. I could write them, I consoled myself.

I began to feel better when we were back on the road and Alex was talking about all the things we would do in Atlanta. By the time we arrived at Blyden's Crossing I was in fine spirits. A strange feeling came over me then,

:143:

scary and exciting at the same time: I was going to see new places. And I was going to ride a train!

All my life I'd watched trains go past, and I'd seen people get on and off them at the station. Once I had helped Miss Etta and Miss Julia lift their suitcases into a day coach when the porter was not there to take them aboard. That was all I'd ever seen of the inside of a train. Of course, tonight we'd ride in a boxcar instead of in a passenger coach. Still, I would be traveling on a train! And I would be going to a city! I felt as happy as that mockingbird we had left singing in the holly tree.

19

Midnight Getaway

Two big crates were on the loading platform. "Good!" said Alex. "The train'll be stopped long enough to load these." He led the way along the track to where he believed the end of the train would stop. There was a small hand-car off to one side, and we sat down on it. We could crouch behind it when the train came in.

"We're on our way!" said Alex.

"Yeah," I said, "but tell me: How come you decided so suddenly that this had to be the night?"

Alex laughed. "Circumstances!"

"What circumstances?"

"Mr. Larson cooperating the way he did."

"You mean he paid you!" I said happily. "I told you he'd live up to his word."

"He didn't exactly pay me," said Alex. "He let me borrow a few things. Hold the light over here, and I'll show you. We're in this together."

I flashed the light onto his knapsack, which he opened just as we heard the ringing sound in the rails. The train was only a few miles away.

"We'd better wait," said Alex, closing the knapsack. But already I had glimpsed what he was about to show me: pocketknives—some of the expensive ones from the special showcase at the store.

"He gave you those?" I asked.

"Not exactly. I borrowed them while he was away. That's how he cooperated: by going to town in late afternoon and leaving me in charge. We can sell the knives on the streets in Atlanta and get us a little money to start with."

"You stole them!" I felt sick.

"Look," said Alex, "he owed me for helping him this past week."

"But not that much." Alex didn't say anything, and finally I added, "Of course, he did make you work off a debt that you didn't owe him." I was thinking of all the weeks Mr. Larson had made Alex work for nothing.

"We'd just as well get that straight too," said Alex. "*You* said it was a debt I didn't owe him!"

"Everybody but me believed you were guilty."

"I *was* guilty," said Alex. I gasped—I couldn't help it —and he laughed as if he had played a good joke on me.

: 146 :

"Well, don't let it choke you!" he said. "Besides, you're the one who said I wasn't guilty, not me."

"Well, you led me to believe you had been accused of something you hadn't done."

"I'd have led anybody to believe it, but nobody else would be led!" He laughed again.

We heard the train whistle and jumped behind the hand-car. "Mr. Larson'll send the police to look for you in Atlanta," I whispered, although there was no need to speak softly. The train was clanging noisily as it went past us.

"He didn't the last time," said Alex.

"Well, he will this time. And even if he doesn't, you'll be run off for sure if you ever want to come back here."

"I never want to come back."

The train slowed to a halt.

"C'mon!" said Alex. "Let's find a place while those crates are being loaded." We rushed to the side of the train. Alex tried the doors of the last three boxcars, but they were locked. "We'll ride the caboose!" he said, and I followed him to it. He swung onto the little observation platform and reached back to give me a hand up.

"I'm not going," I said.

He seemed surprised; maybe I was too. After all, hadn't I always been so determined, once I had decided to do something, that I never changed my mind?

"Suit yourself," said Alex.

"Stay here!" I said. "I'll help you put the knives back, and everything will be all right. Come on, change your mind!"

"Change your own mind," he said sharply. We were both silent a moment, then he added, "Come on, Cowboy! Go with me. You're the only real friend I've ever had."

The train lunged forward, and I jumped to the side. It made two more clanging jerks before starting away slowly. "Good luck!" I said, walking alongside the caboose. There was still time for me to jump aboard.

"Same to you!" Alex reached in his pocket and took out something. "Here," he said, "do what you will with this." He flipped a coin to me, which I almost failed to catch. In the moonlight there was no mistaking that the coin was Cousin Edgar's gold piece.

"But Young stole this!"

"He took the blame," said Alex, "and I took the gold piece. Ol' Young was in the wrong place at the right time —for me—and too stupid to know what was going on!"

Stunned, I looked down at the coin and tried to think of what to say. When I looked up, it was too late to say anything. The train was down the tracks and Alex, at the end of the caboose, looked as if he were floating away . . . like a ghost.

I went back to the depot and sat on the freight platform while I sorted things out in my mind. At first, I was too mad to think clearly. I would be in for trouble; that much I knew. Pa's belt would get a workout. Also, I'd have to do lots of extra jobs in the months ahead. I would do the chores for Miss Etta and Miss Julia, and probably I'd have to work for Mr. Larson too. The only good thing I could think of was that Cousin Edgar, when I'd returned the gold piece to him, would be glad that "Lettie's boy" had not taken it.

Maybe there was another good thing: maybe I had learned something! I didn't plan to go around distrusting people because of Alex, but I sure would be more careful. Since I'd been fooled so easily by him, I guess I wasn't ready to go out on my own after all. Too tired to worry about it, I lay back on the freight platform. Soon I was asleep. When I awoke the moon was down but the sky was beginning to lighten around the edges, and I headed home. Everything was deathly quiet. It was strange to be out at this hour, which was neither night nor day. A rabbit hopped across the road in front of me, and I jumped as if I had met a bear.

Day was beginning to break when I started past Big Will's place. There was a shape out near the road that appeared to be a small tree. Then I realized that it was moving. In the faint light I saw that it was Big Will, carrying milking pails, on his way to the barn. He stopped when he heard my footsteps.

"It's me: Wilkin," I called.

"You're out powerful early," he said, walking out nearer the road. "Ain't nothing wrong, is there?"

"No," I said, "everything's fine." It was a silly answer to give him. Nobody walked down the road at daybreak just for the fun of it. "To tell you the truth, Big Will," I said, "I almost ran away."

"Aw, Wilkin!" he said, sounding genuinely concerned. "How come you're not happy here?"

"It's not that I'm not happy here," I said, trying to